I DI
BED OF ROSES

Angie,
May
we
All
Die
in a
Bed
of
Roses.

KEVIN STRANGE

EDITED BY SEAN FERRARI

KEVINTHESTRANGE.COM

Other books by Kevin Strange:

Robamapocalypse
Cotton Candy
Last Gig on Planet Earth and other Strange Stories (stories)
McHumans
Vampire Guts in Nuke Town
Holey Matrimony (Kindle exclusive)
Loch Ness Lay (Kindle exclusive)
Murder Stories for your Brain Piece (stories)
Computerface
The Humans Under The Bed
The Witch Who Fucked Christmas (website exclusive)
Texas Chainsaw Mantis
All The Toxic Waste From My Heart (stories)

Kevin The Strange HQ
St. Louis, Mo

www.kevinthestrange.com

ISBN-13: 978-1544051659
ISBN-10: 1544051654

AUTHOR'S NOTE:

I wrote this book during a week-long writing marathon alongside the Godfather of Bizarro fiction, Carlton Mellick III. Together we spent long hours deconstructing writing method, story, character. We watched Jean Claude Van Damme movies on VHS and deconstructed them as well.

But mostly we wrote our books.

I sat up there in the loft of a cabin for many days with no phone or internet, totally cut off from the outside world, except for the mountain men and women that populate the small coastal village in Oregon in which we were writing.

I've marathoned books inside supposedly haunted hotels, fleabag motels, my own bedrooms, and inside fast food restaurants, but this was the first time I've done a marathon with another person. I have to say it was a really great experience having someone to meet up with at the end of a long, grueling 10-12 hour writing day to discuss your frustrations, triumphs and overall progress. It really helped stave off the burnout and keep me excited for the next writing day.

There were some parts of this book—the first third,

for example—that came very quickly and easily. Characters developed from nothing into fully fleshed-out people before my eyes in a very short amount of time. Other parts of the book were a slog to get through and took many hours of laying around the loft, staring out at the rosebushes in front of the house across the street, and long walks along the beach before I was able to crack through them and continue.

Some of the scenes gave me goosebumps. Some of them made me cry. It was an emotionally taxing book; but then, all of them are.

This book was informed and inspired by a lot of things: The Richard Linklater film *Before Sunrise*, the Tarantino-written *True Romance*, the Japanese splatter films *Meatball Machine* and *Tetsuo the Iron Man*. But as I rounded the bend on the final third of the book, I realized that, more than anything, I was telling the story of my first real relationship. The first time I felt madly and irreversibly in love.

We were teenagers in high school and her parents hated my parents. We were forbidden to see each other and had to keep finding elaborate ways to spend time together. She would say she was going for a walk and I'd pick her up several blocks from her house, spend an hour with her, then drop her off at the same spot. Or her friends would pick her up and drop her off at my house so we could spend evenings together before I would take her back to whichever friend's house she'd told her parents she was staying the night at.

In the time before cell phones were cheap and easily affordable by everyone, we even developed a secret code with a pager I bought her. I would page her with whatever phone number I was at at the time, and she would call me from her parents' house so that I wouldn't have to call and risk getting her mom or dad on the phone.

Inevitably we would get caught in some nonsense lie and she would get grounded for long months, just for being seen with me out in a car or at a restaurant. Our relationship was very stressful and complicated because of those barriers and limitations, but it did nothing to abate my love for her. I would have done anything to be with that girl, and yet, in the end, as these things always play out, the exhaustion of hiding her boyfriend from her family became too much for a teenage girl to mess with and she ended it, breaking my heart worse than any woman has broken it since.

I still resent her parents. Small town folk who, sure, were just looking out for their daughter's best interests—but what if they'd left us alone? Would our relationship still have burned out? Would we have stayed together? Would I have married my high school sweetheart? Settled down early? Had kids? Would there ever have been a Kevin Strange, the author and filmmaker, if my life had taken that course?

This book is about what-ifs. It's about taking chances. It's about not letting some outside force dictate our emotions for us.

I still love that girl. We're both adults in our thirties now. She has a home and a family and a career. I went on to love many women after her. In fact, I think I might be falling in love with someone right now, which is why I chose to write a romance novel out here on the edge of the country.

But I have never again loved as strongly, never as totally. Never fucked someone as passionately, nor cried as hard when it was all over. She will always be my first love. This book is kind of about her. It's kind of about our relationship.

I kind of still love her.

Kevin Strange
11:49AM May 4th 2016
Oregon Coast

DEDICATION:

This book is for my first love and me, in some other reality on some alternate timeline—the one where we stayed together and our love never faded. This book is for you two. I'm proud of you for sticking it through, despite the odds.

Special Thanks:

I couldn't do what I do without the help of Sean Ferrari, Katie Ferrari, Jeremy Daniels, Ty Bechel, all the Strangeheads I've gained along the way, the Hack Minions who've stayed by my side through it all and each and every one of you reading this right now.

Patrons:

SL Koch, Jeremy Maddux and Shane Vozar

NOW

CHAPTER 1
REVENGE

My hand bursts through the soft earth.

Frantic, I grope the air, feeling for something—
anything—to grab hold of. I find purchase against the
thorny branch of a rosebush. Ignoring the pain, I yank,
pulling the rest of myself closer to the surface, shredding
my hand in the process.

I scream. No sound emerges. My mouth is full of
dirt.

My other arm breaks the surface. I paw the fresh
soil, raking deep lines in the soft earth, pulling rose petals
into the ground with me.

My head is free, my shoulders.

I cough and spit and choke, clearing my nose and
mouth of rich, fertile muck.

I do not scream again.

It's dark outside, hot. Summer. The sky booms with
heat thunder, threatening a storm.

There is a storm inside me. Anger, betrayal, hatred,
and worst of all love. Still love.

Even now. I still love her.

My legs breach the shallow grave. I rise up to my

knees and breathe moist, dank air. I wait.

I am weak. My body shakes. How long had I been under there?

Why am I alive?

When my eyes adjust enough to see the silhouette of the farmhouse against the jet black night sky, I rise to my feet, steady myself and move slowly in that direction. My foot strikes something amongst the rosebushes.

The shovel used to dig my grave.

I take it in my hands, let its weight pull against my aching bones and plod toward the house.

Toward her.

The greenhouse door slams. "No no no. Not supposed to happen! No no no!"

The lumbering figure, all dirty overalls and sweat-soaked hair, shambles toward me. "Stay in the rose garden. Stay in the ground. That's where you belong now. That's your home. That's—"

I smash him in the face, crying out in exertion. It takes all of my energy to raise the shovel above my head and bring it back down. He drops, hands raising to the split in the skin that now runs from his chin to his forehead. I swing a second time, crushing his gloved hands, his nose. Teeth.

Again I hit him. His breathing is loud and erratic, his head a smear of shining black against the darkness. Turning the shovel point-down, I thrust, cleaving his head from his neck, silencing him.

The screen door of the farmhouse slams.

"Luke?"

Even now, after everything—after what she and her brother did to me—she is the most beautiful creature I've ever laid eyes on. Her long, tendril-like hair billows back as she rushes toward us, fiery crimson even in the black of night. I redouble my grip on the handle of my shovel. I breathe deep, strained breaths; not because I'm physically exhausted (which I am), but because the sight of her still takes my breath away.

Maggie. My love.

"Luke, what—"

She stops short when she sees me, when she sees her brother's corpse on the ground.

"Brian."

She loves me. Still. I see it. Penetrating the darkness. In the glint of her eyes. Her face betrays her, its expression the same as that first night we met. That awe. That infatuation.

She loves me still.

I smash her. I weep. I bring the shovel down on her twitching body again and again. I want to erase her. I want to erase the love, the hurt, the agony. Silence the storm in me.

It does not diminish one single bit.

Thunder crashes overhead. Lightning. In that flash I see the red. See her face. Her eyes. Small sounds escape what's left of her mouth.

I smash until those things are no more.

The rain starts as I finish with Maggie. I wipe it out of my eyes as I start toward the house.

Toward her mother.

My name is Brian Sully, and I died in that bed of roses.

THEN

CHAPTER 2
MY LIFE ON THE COAST

Moving to the Oregon coast was supposed to make life better, not worse. Rockwood Village was nothing more than a small strip of restaurants, antique shops, and a tiny neighborhood east of the coastal highway.

It was the perfect place for my exile. The perfect place for me to disappear.

I am Brian Sully, cult horror filmmaker. Not a household name, but notable enough to be considered famous in the right circles. I found success very early, when I was barely twenty-one years old. I wrote and directed a short film based on the works of legendary pulp horror writer H.P. Lovecraft. I submitted it to a film festival and won first prize: A trip to LA to meet with producers and the chance to direct another Lovecraft based film, this time with a modest (yet significant) budget.

It did well enough to launch my career as a low budget horror filmmaker, a career that lasted for more than a decade. But the constant grind, the stress, the politics and the meager paychecks left me disenfranchised, tired and jaded. After my seventh feature film as a writer and director, at 33 years of age, I took my ball and went home.

It wasn't only that. God I wish it was only that. There was also a scandal. The kind of scandal that even a schlocky B-movie director like me couldn't escape. A sex scandal.

As innocuous as I may have thought it was at the time, it put a mark on my name. A series of graphic pictures I shared with the leading lady of my last film along with several emails describing in careful detail exactly what I wanted to do to her with the subject of the pictures.

We hit it off at first, Julia and I. But by the end of the third week of production, we couldn't stand each other. She made my life a living hell for the remaining shoot dates, and I did my best to make her scenes as physically and emotionally grueling as possible.

The film turned out great. The tension between us came across as genuine terror and anger on screen. It was by far her best performance. But she wasn't about to let it go. She couldn't quit the movie and risk her own reputation, so she got her revenge in another way.

She took to the internet. She shared the images and emails I'd sent her the first week of production when we were getting along great. I was labeled a pervert and shamed across the horror community message boards and websites.

My career was ruined. Julia had won.

So I quit. Saved my friends and colleagues the embarrassment of having to justify working with me again. I cashed in my savings and left the Midwest in favor of the Pacific Northwest. I moved to Rockwood, bought a small cabin, took a job at the tiny grocery located along the highway and started work on my first horror novel.

I thought I could get away from the nonsense of the horror community bickering, infighting, backstabbing, gossiping and, yes, sex scandals. Mine wasn't the first scandal, and certainly not the last. It was as if the community needed an annual sacrifice to purge its members, keep its numbers low. Keep the beast from bloating.

I thought I could blend in with regular people again. Not be recognized in diners by groups of horror kids wanting autographs while I tried to eat an omelet. Not have those autograph signings always turn awkward when the kids asked me why I didn't direct features anymore.

I was wrong.

"Oh my god! Brian, is this your dick?"

I was stocking macaroni and cheese boxes when Anna ran up and stuck her phone in my face.

My blood ran cold. I dropped a box of mac and cheese the hard shells bursting on the floor at my feet. I took the girl's phone, expecting to see those graphic images I'd shared over a decade before.

It was my dick. But not from the sex scandal pictures.

I'd appeared in a scene in that first short film I'd made. The one that launched my career.

Sons of Dagon.

In the scene, my on-screen girlfriend and I make love on a small boat when creatures from the sea capsize the boat and drown us. In the scene, we're both nude.

I looked at Anna incredulously. She was a mousey girl with a wispy, dirty blonde pony tail, glasses and big blue braces. All of nineteen years old.

"Why are you showing me this?" I knelt down to clean up the spilled macaroni. As awkward as it was to be staring at a picture of my genitals at my place of employment, I couldn't help but feel a tremendous sense of relief. Even after all this time, I was still just as emotionally triggered by the events that had lead to my early retirement from film as I was when the whole awful thing unfolded.

"I didn't know you made porno movies!" She giggled and grinned at me. The other counter girl, Courtney, laughed from the checkout. Even Steve, the middle-aged grocery manager, smiled from across the store.

I couldn't tell if Anna wanted to fuck me or was just being obnoxious for the sake of it. I'd been in Rockwood for ten years. At 43, I didn't exactly look at the counter girls as dating material. Truth be told, the sex scandal had left me jaded and unwilling (if not downright unable) to put trust into any sort of meaningful relationship. I hadn't even been on a single date in the decade since I'd been shunned by the horror community.

That only made the brazen flirting of a teenage girl —or whatever the hell she was doing by waving my own dick in my face—all the more awkward.

"Please put that away." I returned to my macaroni boxes, embarrassed. What else was I supposed to say? I was being sexually harassed with my own dick by a teenage girl.

This was some kind of karmic revenge for the Julia emails...

"You're just mad cause it's small!"

Courtney laughed out loud and even Steve snorted at Anna's obnoxious taunting.

"It's not—" I almost took the bait. Almost engaged in a debate about the size of my penis with a grocery store girl less than half my age. I pushed past her and walked across the store to where Steve leaned against the front window. The store was empty, save us employees. It was still the off-season, even though the weather had already warmed up farther inland. The waters way up here came down from the arctic, keeping them cold nearly all year round. Only the locals stuck around Rockwood when the water was cold.

"Please make her stop."

Steve chuckled. He was a mountain man in training. A true Oregon native. His bristly black mustache would eventually turn into a full gray beard and he would lose his teeth. His interests were fishing, the grocery store, and nothing else. "You're the one put the movie on the internet."

A full length video of *Sons of Dagon* was on my official website along with the trailers and some scenes from my feature films. The site hadn't been up updated in years, but I'd left it active for posterity's sake. A final act of defiance after I left the community. They could smear my name, put a pox on my career, but they could not erase the art I'd made. Now I regretted that decision.

I took off my apron. "I'll see you tomorrow, Steve."

He was still grinning. Steve was a local. So were Anna and Courtney. Native Pacific Northwesterners. They'd never traveled much outside of the mountains, and their intellect reflected that fact. "What? You've still got two hours left on your shift!"

"Take it up with Anna."

I walked back to my cabin two blocks away on Easy Street (I'd taken that as a good omen when I'd moved to Rockwood. Life on East Street—now it felt like a mockery).

I was still seething both in anger and embarrassment from Anna's harassment as I cracked open a beer and sat down at my computer. The manuscript for my new novel, *The True Origins of The Deep Ones,* was open on the desktop. I sipped my beer and focused in on the book to take my mind off the weird events of the day.

I read over the last few paragraphs I'd written. They were awful. The truth was, I was a crappy author. As a filmmaker, my style was visually distinct. I'd made my mark with visceral slime and latex monsters set against stark colored backgrounds. My scripts were often little more than an excuse to get pretty girls naked and covered with gore and goo—a fetish that would ironically both launch my career and spell its demise. As a novelist, this type of storytelling came off to me as cheap and unrewarding.

I sat back and drank the rest of my beer in one swig. In my mind I saw Anna holding her phone, waggling my own dick at me again. I tried to imagine her naked. I slipped my hand in my pants and rubbed my cock. It wasn't small. I wasn't any kind of size champion, but I wasn't small.

I pictured myself rubbing my erection against Anna's smooth face, telling her just that.

I know, Mr. Sully. I just wanted you to prove it. I pictured Anna taking my erection into her mouth, careful not to scrape it against her braces.

Her braces.

I took my hand out of my pants. Disgusting. What the fuck was wrong with me?

Perhaps I was the pervert my film-making community had painted me as. Perhaps the world of art was better off without me in it, harassing and stalking all the pretty actresses.

I sighed. It was dark outside. I decided to take a stroll across the beach to clear my mind.

I took the long way as to avoid the grocery. The moon was full and low, casting its brilliant pale light against the endless waves. I took off my shoes and left them atop a picnic table in the parking lot. I loved the way the sand felt against my bare feet, even on a brisk night like this. The cold made me feel alive.

I walked out to the shoreline, staring into the vastness before me, wincing against the freezing water as the tide gently broke against my skin. Alone out there, just me and the ocean, I thought about Lovecraft and his monsters that dwelled beneath the surface of the water. Lovecraft, my muse. I'd made a career off of the world and the monsters he'd dreamed up. A man long dead before I'd been born. A ghost beckoning me to create in his image. A dead god.

I felt empty inside. I'd written five novels since I'd been in Rockwood. No one had read them. No one had read them because I never showed them to anyone. They were bad. I was a bad writer. Plain and simple. I'd walked away from what I was good at. Great at. My movie career was long dead. My plans to retire and hide away from the world to write books had failed.

What did I have left?

The tide pulled harder against my bare feet, ankle-high now. The waves got bigger, stronger. I'd have to move inland soon or I'd be swept into the sea.

I didn't move.

I stood transfixed, gazing out into nothing, searching my mind for a reason to retreat to dry land. Water crashed against my shins. Calf-high now.

What was back there? Anna and Steve? The Grocery? My crappy books?

My contacts in the film world were more than relieved when I'd announced my retirement. I hadn't heard from anyone I'd made a movie with in a decade. Not my actors. Not my editors.

I'd felt nothing but numbness when I'd gotten word that Julia had overdosed on drugs and died on a straight to DVD soft-core porno set five years prior. Her career had not taken off the way she'd expected it to after our scandal. It seemed to mark her as difficult to work with as much as it had marked me as a pervert.

Julia Stine was dead. Brian Sully was already as good as dead. Why not just be finished with it?

My phone rang, breaking that dark train of thought.

I jogged up out of the water back to the table with my shoes on it.

"Brian Sully, how can I help you?"

It was my producer, Barry. He'd been with me from the beginning. From *Sons of Dagon* all the way up through my final feature. He'd been like a brother to me.

We were like soldiers who'd survived war. We'd quit the business at the same time.

He assured me he'd made all the movies he wanted to make. That he'd saved smart, and that our exits were only a coincidence. But I knew. I knew people couldn't mention Barry without mentioning Brian Sully. We were a team.

And then we were nothing.

He opened a car lot; I became a stock boy.

"Come home, buddy."

It was the twentieth anniversary of *Sons of Dagon*. A Lovecraftian film festival in Cincinnati, Ohio had contacted Barry and asked if he could get me to come and present the film. Do a Q and A. Sign autographs.

The festival promoter had to be crazy. No one had asked me a single time to make a public appearance since the scandal. Not once. Had time been kind to my name after I'd faded away? Or was this some shyster just looking to make horror headlines by booking a controversial name that would get the internet outraged?

"You know I don't do that shit anymore, Barry."

But the truth was, a festival sounded good. Maybe the world had forgotten about Brian Sully's lewd pictures. Maybe a weekend with my friends and fans was exactly what I needed to reinvigorate my spirit. I wasn't looking forward to another summer season on the coast again, anyway. Too many tourists. Too many human beings in general. For someone trying to hide from the world, I'd picked a pretty crappy spot to do so.

"Come *on*, brother!" Barry said in his smoothest car-salesman-pitch voice. There's a LOT of money to be made! Don't make me make it without you."

I hesitated. "What about... you know..."

"Water under the bridge, Bud! Nobody cares about that shit anymore. It happened ten years ago! Ancient stuff!"

What was the worst that could happen? I'd already

lived through my sex scandal once. I'd just been standing in the fucking ocean contemplating suicide. Even if a crowd of liberal crazies showed up to protest the Lovecraftian pervert's movie screening, I could always blow my fucking brains out in front of them and really make some headlines.

I agreed to attend the show.

Walking back to the cabin, I stopped inside the grocery and tendered my resignation. I figured between the money I'd squirreled away from working at the store and what the festival had agreed to pay me, I'd be able to afford the mortgage on the cabin for at least six months. If I still didn't know what to do with my life after that, well, my stock boy job would be the least of my problems.

I booked a flight and packed, stopping back at the beach one last time before I left Rockwood. Several families were out there on the shore, parents braving the frigid waves to frolic in the water with their children.

I smiled, drove away, and never saw the ocean again.

CHAPTER 3
THE FESTIVAL

I stood in the hotel bathroom, shaving, wishing I'd never left the coast.

This had been a mistake.

I'd been in hotels just like this. Spoke at festivals just like this. Maybe this very same hotel room at this very same festival years before. Those days were a blur of long highways, loose women and strong whiskey. Barry and I did these things all year long when we weren't in production on a film. We'd make more money on the festival and convention circuit than we made from our films, usually.

And we'd both grown to hate ourselves because of it. The lure of beautiful women throwing themselves at us, sometimes in twos and threes, was... well, it was fantastic. Often times their boyfriends and husbands provided us the drugs and alcohol while they waited in the lobby, or, on really wild nights, would even watch us fuck their women. It made us feel like rock stars. Like kings.

But it robbed us of our souls. I blamed our drug-addled lifestyle, my cavalier attitude, for my eventual downfall. I was so genuinely shocked when Julia had come out publicly accusing me of sexually harassing her on set, that at first I thought it was a joke. Barry and I had done so much more with so many other women—done so much more *to* so many other women—without ever receiving a single complaint. I was completely jaded to life outside of the little bubble we'd created for ourselves.

Neither Berry nor I had married by the time our twenties turned into our thirties. Relationships required patience, commitment, compromise. Why mess with all of that nonsense when pretty young girls with painted black hair and tattoos of our monster creations would snort cocaine off our cocks?

Now there I stood again. Back in the belly of the beast. Everything that had built me, that had destroyed me. I was vibrating from nervousness. It felt like a mistake, like a recovering addict in a crack house.

A knock came at the bathroom door. "You ready for this, buddy?"

Barry wore a black t-shirt with the *Sons of Dagon* logo sprawled across it in bright green dripping letters resembling seaweed and "Twenty Years Dead and Dreaming" written below it.

He handed me an identical one to wear.

Barry was the showman. He'd had the shirts printed up the week before the show—five hundred of them, and he would surely sell them all this weekend. He knew how to market our movies, how to make us money. Without him, I'd have never been able to afford to shoot a single frame of film.

"Why are we doing this again?"

Barry patted me on my freshly-shaved face and laughed. "You're gonna do fine, buddo. We've done this a million times. It's like riding a bike. Once you're a famous cult movie director, you're always a famous cult movie director."

Once you're labeled a sexually deviant pervert,

you're always a sexually deviant pervert, I thought.

***

I presented the film, just like I had countless times before. Barry was right; once I was on the stage with the mic in hand, the words, wit, and humor came right back to me. Playing the crowd and answering questions with snarky, jokey retorts that had the sold-out auditorium of horror-hounds howling with approval felt like second nature to me.

Yet I still felt terrified. Kept waiting for the other shoe to drop. Waiting for the next question to be the one that brought the whole thing crumbling down. "Have you anything to say about Julia Stine's accusations of sexual harassment on the set of your last film?" "What would she think of your little comeback party were she still with us today?"

But those questions never came. It was almost like this group of cult film lovers was protecting me from my past. That my time away had been time served. That I'd paid my penalty up there in the Pacific Northwest. They'd built me up, torn me down, and were ready to see me rise once more.

For the first time in a long, long time, I felt like everything was going to be alright.

I stood in the back with Barry as the film played. I'd seen it so many times, it didn't even seem like a film anymore. The narrative made no sense, the creature effects were cheap and flawed. The editing was choppy and laughable.

I looked at Barry. He had that goofy grin on his face he always had when we screened our films. I'd asked him in the past why he always smiled like that, and he'd told me all he thinks about when we do screenings is how much money he just made.

"Why'd you quit?" I whispered to him while a

floppy breasted blonde on screen was chewed to pieces by a sea monster with three face tentacles that resembled big green dicks.

"Huh?" Barry tore his eyes away from the jiggling tits and leaned closer to me.

"You love this shit. Why'd you give it up when I did? Why didn't you just keep making movies? It was me, wasn't it? Tell me the truth. You quit because of what happened."

I hadn't spoken aloud about the incident in a decade. My mouth was dry. The words felt like mothballs rolling off my tongue.

As a response, he pulled out his phone and opened up his photo gallery app. He turned the screen toward me and slowly flipped through an album titled "The Little Family."

"You haven't changed, Brian," he whispered, slowly swiping through the gallery of pictures. "Still think this world is all about you."

He'd stayed here in the Midwest, married an old high school sweetheart and bought a house in our home town. The pictures showed his three-year-old daughter Audrey playing on the swingset he'd built in his backyard. Still more photos showed his pretty wife Barbara with their newborn boy, Barry Jr., who'd been born just four months prior to the festival. There were pictures of birthday parties, wedding photos, family vacations.

"I quit for them, buddo. Not you. Not your little scandal. They're my life now." He looked at me quizzically. "That's why I did this in the first place—so I could have some fun and make enough money to start a family. Why the fuck did you do it?"

I downed my whiskey.

***

"You're the most critically underrated horror director of all time, Mr. Sully. I just want you to know that."

I was seated at a table outside the screening room. A banner with my face, name and covers of my movies hung behind me, while copies of the movies and glossy 8x10 pictures of still images of the monsters and babes from the flicks at various price points sat facing away from me.

The kid in front of me was shaking while I signed his DVDs of *Sons of Dagon* and several of my other movies. He had piercings in his face and wore a goofy baseball cap with a big eyeball on the top, and some kind of fanged mouth on the underside of the brim.

"Thanks, man." What more could I say? I'd heard this kind of shit so many times. It always made me feel good, but I couldn't help but think that these horror fans knew the truth about my past and were just coddling me, protecting me from reality like some kind of cuddly horror mascot that couldn't possibly be dangerous now that he's older. They didn't know about Anna and the grocery store. They didn't know about my crappy novels or the night at the ocean when I'd almost killed myself.

Maybe I'd overreacted about Julia's choice to publicly shame me. Maybe I should have settled down like Barry. Not been so dramatic by quitting the business and moving to the coast. Maybe I should have tried to let it blow over. Gotten married...

It's not that I didn't love women. That was the problem: I loved *women*. Never one woman. Not since I was a teenager, anyway.

Making movies had always taken up far too much of my time for any relationship to ever take firm hold. There had been fierce, defiant women who had thought that their particular brand of seduction would be enough to lure me away from the filmmaking lifestyle. But there were always more women, and more movies to make

—'til Julia ruined the whole thing.

But had she? Had she really? Sitting there signing movies for horror dorks and their hot girlfriends with looks of awe and reverence on their faces gave me pause. Had I just been looking for an excuse to quit? If I'd stayed the course, would I have ended up just like Barry?

I looked over at him, wheeling and dealing t-shirts at the table next to me. He'd always had a sweaty sheen, a manic disposition that made him look nervous. That was gone now. He looked relaxed. He looked fulfilled.

A bouncy skinny girl with full sleeve tattoos, huge gauged ear plugs and eye makeup so thick it made her look like a possessed demon stepped up to the table next. Her beefy boyfriend stood next to her carrying bags of horror memorabilia.

"Hi, Mr. Sully! I'm your biggest fan! I LOVED *Bride of Dagon*! Will you sign my tits?"

I seized up, awkward smile still on my face as I glanced back and forth between them. Was this it? Would this slutty looking girl post my picture all over the internet calling me a creepy perverted scumbag?

"I- uh. I don't think—"

"Oh, it's cool, man. She's gonna get it turned into a tattoo over there." The boyfriend waved toward another section of the film festival with long tables full of tattoo artists.

Reluctantly, I removed the cap from my pen as the girlfriend yanked the collar of her shirt down to give me easy access to her breasts.

I scribbled my name.

Her boyfriend looked more excited about my autograph on her chest than she did....

***

After the screening, I left Barry at the hotel bar. Drinking at the same venue as the festival was like working another show, only this time the fans didn't ask for an autograph and leave, they wanted to buy you drinks and hang out. This was a great way to get drunk for free, but that's not what I was after.

I needed to think.

I wandered down the road until I found a shitty looking dive bar. Shitty enough that I didn't think anyone from the festival would be inside. I was right.

It was a redneck bar. Bull riding and UFC played on the television screens and country music blared from the jukebox. The likelihood of being recognized in here was slim.

I saddled up next to the bar and ordered a beer and a whiskey. A man old enough to be my grandfather drank to my left. The stool to my right was empty.

I drank.

The violence on the television screens washed over me as I swallowed another shot, wondering what my end game was.

What was next? A comeback film? Was I really considering that? What else was left?

I thought about the beach again. Thought about what would have happened if my phone hadn't rang. If Barry's call hadn't pulled me back from the tide.

Suicide was never something I'd considered when I was making movies. I was having too goddamn much fun. But putting the brakes on that, retreating to the coast, staying single and writing those god-awful books had faded life's wonder and luster. Did I want to be this jaded, empty vessel for forty, fifty more years?

I thought of Barry's photo album. Tried to picture myself in his place: Baby boy, beautiful little girl, perfect wife. Would that make me happy? Would that complete Brian Sully?

"Two whiskeys, please."

The voice alone was enough to make me and the old man next to me turn our heads.

She wore a slinky sundress with a pink and yellow flower pattern on green material. Her voluminous scarlet hair hung down past her shoulders, ending in wild tips like blades of red grass. Her left leg was kicked forward as she leaned into the counter, giving both of us men a clear view of the contours of her legs and ass. We liked what we saw.

When she had her drinks, she turned from the bar, leaned her back against it and downed both shots, one after the other, her thick lips emanating a satisfied smack as she wiped her mouth. She turned and dropped the shot glasses back on the counter. She slyly glared at the both of us out of the corner of her eye without turning her head the slightest bit.

"You boys gonna eyeball fuck me all night, or is one of you gonna grow a pair and buy the next round?"

That's how I met her.

That's how I met Maggie.

CHAPTER 4
HOME

After the festival, I didn't return to the coast. I decided to ride home with Barry. I wanted to spend some time with my mother; at least that's what I told him.

Barry played the newest Iron Maiden album in the car and gleefully chattered on about all the money he'd made off the shirts and festival-exclusive twentieth anniversary *Sons of Dagon* DVDs.

I didn't speak ten words the entire trip home. My mind was other places.

My mind was on *her*.

My father had passed away a decade before, during a brief period when Barry and I had lived in LA and were deep in the throes of cocaine addiction. He died suddenly of a heart attack while working on his truck in the driveway. My mother had found him. I didn't come home for the funeral—I had been too fucked up and too far away to fully comprehend how badly that had messed her up.

When we'd snorted all of our money from our latest feature, *Cyber Kraken and the Lords of Cthuhlu*, we'd decided to move back home—him with his parents, me with my mom—while we sorted out our drug addiction and worked on financing our next low budget horror film.

To that point, I'd never seen my mother so much as drink a beer with dinner. But when I flew home from LA, she was a full-on drunk. That was ten years ago.

It had only gotten worse since.

Late that Sunday night, Barry dropped me off in front of my mother's house. I immediately knew something was wrong. The grass in the front yard was completely overgrown. I climbed the porch steps and saw a notification from the city posted on the front door stating that she'd been fined five hundred dollars for multiple ordinance violations after complaints about the state of her lawn.

I snatched the notice off the door and used the key under the mat to let myself in.

I found her sleeping on the couch. Wine bottles completely covered the coffee table. The house smelled. The air was thick with the pungent aroma of cat piss and rotten food. Several mangy looking felines circled my legs and cried until I followed them into the kitchen and poured them some fresh food and water. At least a week's worth of dishes sat unwashed in the sink.

I returned to the living room and pulled the quilt off the back of the couch, covering my mom. I brushed the damp hair out of her face. She'd gone completely gray since my last visit. She looked a decade older than her sixty-one years.

Quietly, I grabbed my luggage and climbed the stairs, entering my old bedroom. I closed the door and removed my laptop from my backpack. I sat at my writing desk and powered it on. I opened up a search engine and typed the words: *Family farms, five hundred mile radius, Cincinnati Ohio.*

***

"You're not too old to have children, you know that, Bry?"

It wasn't quite 12pm yet, so my mother was still sober (well, as sober as she ever got). She was comprehensible until noon. That's when the heavy drinking started.

I'd gotten up early, filled up the lawn mower and taken care of the front and back lawns. She'd woken from her bender and crawled off the couch after I'd come back in and showered.

I ate my cereal, ignoring her.

"Your father never gave me a brother or sister for you. This house is so big. There's plenty of room for some little kiddos running around. We've got such a big yard..."

She trailed off, drinking her coffee, smoking her cigarette. She'd never smoked when my dad was alive, either.

"You should go out, Ma. Make some friends," I said between bites of Captain Crunch. "Meet some people."

"A boyfriend, you mean. I should get a boyfriend. Get remarried, right? You'd like that, wouldn't you?"

I looked over at her, spoon still in my mouth. Shit.

She was crying.

"I only ever loved your father! This is his house. There will never be another man living here not named Michael Allen Sully, I can promise you that, young man!"

"Ma, I'm borrowing the car. I stocked the fridge with food and wine. I don't know when I'll be home. And please don't cry. You know it breaks my heart."

I kissed her on the forehead and took the car keys from the hook by the door. I paused, wishing there was something I could do or say that would fix this awful thing, but she'd turned her back to me, already going for the wine in the fridge.

I shut the door behind me.

When my father passed, I used the majority of the

money from my next three features to pay off the mortgage on their house so my mother wouldn't have to move. In some ways, I think that was the worst thing I could have done. My father's life insurance had left her enough money to live comfortably, so she'd quit her job. With the mortgage paid, she was left alone to sit. To dwell. To rot.

Once in the car, I took out my cell and dialed the phone number written on the notebook in front of me.

No answer.

I took my pen and circled Grant's Farm on my list of independently operated farms. There were thirty on the page. I'd started with over 150 farms, eliminating all but the thirty with either no listed phone numbers, or those that did not pick up my call.

I entered the GPS coordinates in my phone. Grant's Family Farm. *Two hundred eighty seven miles to your destination*, the stern female voice said.

I had to see her again.

I had to see Maggie.

CHAPTER 5
THE BAR

"I'm guessing you're a fan of my movies."

"Huh?"

I was drunk. Not wasted, but I was working on it. I was on my fifth beer, drinking it like it was my first. "Your tattoos. They look like Deep Ones. The shit from my movies."

"I don't know what you're talking about. I drew these."

I was talking to Maggie. I'd practically had to fight the old guy on the stool next to me to buy her another shot of whiskey and a beer. He'd called for the bartender first, but she'd ignored his drinks and instead introduced herself to me. We made our way over to a quiet table in the corner, leaving the old man sulking in his drink, cussing me under his breath.

Maggie's left arm was covered shoulder to wrist in intricate graywash black and white pictures of snarling aquatic monsters with sharp talons, webbed claws, bat wings, and more tentacles than I could count.

"I'm sorry, I uh. Wow." I chuckled, embarrassed. "I'm kind of a big deal out here this weekend," I said mockingly, try to save face.

"You don't look special to me," Maggie said, smirking.

"Ouch. I deserved that one."

She leaned in, touching her shoulder to mine, giggling. Her teeth were big and white. Her full lips formed around them, creating the most gorgeous smile I'd ever seen. Or maybe I was wasted. Or horny. Or both.

"Those creatures," I said, tearing my eyes away from her mouth, trying to clear my head. "They look like the monsters from my movies. They look like Lovecraft's creations."

"Sorry. They're Maggie-craft creations," she said, shaking her head back and forth, playfully challenging me to question her tattoos' authenticity again.

I noticed then for the first time just how blue her eyes were. Clear like marbles, slightly reddish in the corners from all the drinking we'd done in the past hour.

"So you make movies, huh? What kind, porno movies?"

My smile faded. I sat still, that same fear rising up inside me. That jolt of anxiety that hit me when Barry had texted me the day Julia Stine had gone public with my emails and pictures.

"What the fuck did you do, man???" is all the text said.

I remembered like it happened yesterday, not ten years ago. I remembered the feeling of helplessness as the horror websites, one after another, posted stories with sensational headlines.

Horror-Porn Director Sends Lewd Photos To Starlet!

Son of Dagon Director Shows Off His Dagon-Dick!

As beautiful as Maggie was, I couldn't shake the fear. I couldn't go through all that again. Julia had seemed so cool on set—just as cool as Maggie was being right then. Hell, Julia had been just as flirty and just as forward as any of the other starlets I'd fucked on my movie sets.

Just another day at the office: Write a smutty monster movie, cast the cutest babes, bang them in my trailer before we'd shoot every day. Nothing was out of the ordinary—not until she went public with my emails. Then suddenly I was a pervert. A sexual deviant of the highest order. Some of the more desperate websites even tried to insinuate that my salacious emails were tantamount to rape.

I was just a guy. Just a young dude surrounded by beautiful women who had no qualms with banging their director to get ahead in their acting careers. A win/win for both of us.

Or was I just making excuses for my insane behavior? The truth is, I couldn't even remember typing up those emails or taking those photos. I'd let my cocaine addiction turn to an alcohol addiction.

Those last couple of features, if I'm being honest with myself, had been carried almost entirely by Barry. He'd never let me list him as co-director, even though he did a tremendous amount of production work on every single movie we'd made. "You're the rockstar. I'm the manager," he'd always tell me. But those last few... Barry made those movies. I was practically on another planet.

What the fuck was I doing here at this stupid bar? With this girl? I was getting myself into trouble all over again and I'd only been in town one day! I started making excuses in my head to leave and go back to the safety of the hotel room. Away from the public. Away from her.

"Hey! Earth to weirdo!" she said, snapping my train of thought. She eyed me slyly. "Say, you're not some wacko religious type, are you?"

"What? No, I-"

Maggie mock-sighed in relief. "Good! My mom's super religious. I hate that shit. Sorry about the porno comment, I was joking."

"No, no it's fine, I wish I made porno," I said,

forcing my anxiety and paranoia to take a backseat. "I'd have a lot more money in the bank if I did."

That caused a whole new giggle fit from my beautiful companion.

There was something about Maggie. Something in her eyes, in her face, in the way she leaned into me. Something in the way she drank her beer, as if she was seducing it.

I wasn't afraid of her like I'd been afraid of practically every woman I'd met in the last ten years. I sensed something in her. Something different. A kind of attraction that transcended the fact that she had a stripper's body and a teenage boy's sense of humor.

Maggie was... different.

"Why don't we talk about you? Fuck what I do. I've been talking about what I do all weekend."

"Farm girl."

"Farm girl, huh? Should have guessed; hick bar and all."

She made a snarling shape with her lips. "I fucking hate country music. I prefer metal."

I made devil horns with my hands and stuck my tongue out, mock headbanging.

She punched my arm.

"I own—well, my *mom* owns—an organic farm."

"Aren't all farms organic?"

"Shut the fuck up!" she said, laughing. "It means we're off the grid. No Monsanto, no GMOs. No chemicals. All natural plants and animals."

I shifted in my seat. This girl was actually interesting, beyond her amazing face and body. My instinct had been correct. I felt relieved that I hadn't gotten up and scampered away when the fear had struck me. "What kinds of animals do you raise?"

She waved her hand in the air, ticking off a mental list. "Chickens, goats, pigs, the occasional stray cat. You know, the usual."

"I've heard that pigs are smarter than dogs. How can you bring yourself to slaughter an animal that answers when you call its name?"

It was her turn to look at me incredulously.

"I'm not judging," I said, putting my hands out in mock defense. "I eat the shit out of bacon. I'm just curious about your attitude. Do you ever feel sorry for the animals?"

She turned toward me, her expression serious for the first time since I'd met her.

Had that only been a few hours ago? It felt like I'd known this wonderful girl for years.

"Try to imagine your life: You work hard, you struggle, you get old, you get sick. What if you were fed the most delicious foods, cared for by the sweetest people, had your every need attended to, but you only got to live for thirty years, and in the end, had one bad day?"

"I'd rather get old," I said.

"Shut up, you know what I mean. Yes it sucks when you get emotionally attached to an animal, but they have the best lives I can provide for them. And once they're dead, I get to eat their flesh." She smiled, wiggling her eyebrows.

I twirled my finger next to my ear, making the crazy sign.

"Seriously though, if you feel nothing when they're gone, their sacrifice was meaningless."

I thought about that while I finished my beer. "Well, sounds like being a sexy farm girl is actually a lot of hard work."

"Ever gotten up at dawn and worked 'til your fuckin' arms felt like they were falling off, your legs were made of concrete, and your back was practically snapped in half, then passed out after dark, only to get up and do it all again the next day?"

"Can't say that I have," I said, smiling.

"Well, it's like that. Every fucking day of my life!"

"I'd like to watch you do that sometime."

"Do what? Work 'til my arms fall off?"

"Yeah, sounds sexy," I said, signaling the waitress for another round. I changed my voice to sound like an old dirty pervert. "All sweaty and shiny and shit. I bet you look real nice wet." I stuck my tongue out and motioned at her with my hands like I was about to grope her.

I hadn't acted like that in years. Being publicly shamed as the biggest pervert in the horror movie community tends to have an impact on your sense of humor. But Maggie... Maggie brought my guard down.

She laughed so loud the women at the booth behind us shot her a dirty look.

"Would you put me in one of your movies?" She sounded out the movies making it sound as sensual and seductive as possible. "Or am I not pretty enough?"

"Fucking hell," I said, taking another drink from my beer. "You're prettier than any of the so-called actresses I ever worked with."

"Really?" she said, unconvinced. "I'm sure you say that to all the girls." She said the last part in a singsong-y voice, putting emphasis on the absolute cliché of a conversation we were suddenly having.

To break from the cheesy banter, I leaned in and said, "Do you really wanna know what I say to all the girls?"

She nodded.

I took her by the hand, looked deep into her eyes and turned on Director Brian mode. Even though I hadn't done it in years, the intensity and passion for directing gorgeous women in strange movies came right back to me.

"Have you ever acted before?"

"Gosh, no, mister," Maggie said, playing coy.

"Modeled? You have this look. I... I can't explain it. When I look at you I just see..."

46

"Nope. Never."

"My god," I said, staring into her face. I traced my finger over her cheeks, her chin, her lips. "My god. You've got it."

"Got what?" she asked, dropping the act. Her question was genuine. She was already falling for my shtick.

"I don't know. I don't know. I just... I have to photograph you. I have to document this. This... *itness*."

"Itness?"

"I'm going to be honest with you. I've directed girls as pretty as you before. But prettiness, that's easy. Get two pretty people together to fuck, and *wham*, pretty babies. But you. You've got this sadness behind your eyes. This haunted look that just... God. Can I say something?"

"Sure."

I shifted in my seat, squaring up even closer to her. "No, I mean—what I'm going to say is going to scare the shit out of you, and I don't blame you one bit if you walk away calling me a creepy fucking weirdo. I don't blame you if you never speak to me again."

"Uh. I... I guess."

I had her now. This was my big spiel. This is what hooked every last one of them into my trap. What allowed me to shoot them totally naked every day of the week for the entirety of my movie shoots without complaint.

"I want to use that pain. I want to use that sadness inside of you. I want to exploit it. To bring it out to the surface and use it, selfishly, in my film. I want to hurt you. Every day for as long as we're making this movie. I want to hurt you and cause you harm. Emotionally, physically. I want to ruin you. I want to change you. If you do this movie with me, you will walk away a different person. I'm going to scar you. You won't look at movies the same way ever again after I'm done with you.

You will hate me after I'm done with you. You'll never want to look me in the face again. And it will be the most important thing you ever do with your life."

"But," I said slyly, finishing my beer. "I don't do that anymore."

"Whoa," Maggie said, eyes wide. "That was fucking intense. I was ready to get naked right here in the bar and let you have your way with me!"

"Yeah, well. It's a gift," I said, shrugging off her compliment.

"If it's such a gift, then why'd you quit?"

I looked at her, not sure why I was acting the way I was tonight. It wasn't the beer—I'd been drunk countless times since the Julia controversy. Maggie made me feel... safe. Like I could literally tell her anything. So I did.

"I wanted to fuck the girl I cast as the lead in my last movie. I was drunk one night in my trailer the first week of shooting, jacking off, thinking about all the nasty things I wanted to do to her and decided, fuck it."

"Fuck it?" Maggie snorted.

"Yeah, fuck it. I got up, grabbed a length of rope from a bag I'd planned to drop off with the prop department the next morning, and tied off the base of my boner and my balls, making my junk a huge purple engorged mess. Then I took a bunch of pictures of it and attached them to an email."

"Jesus fucking christ!" Maggie said, covering her mouth to try to stifle her laughter. "Why the fuck would you tie up your *dick*?"

"That's not the best part," I said. I decided to just tell her the whole thing.

I'd never told anyone this out loud before. Not a single person; not even Barry had heard it directly from me. Oh, everyone knew what the emails said. Everyone had gotten a nice good look at my bound and gagged purple pecker. But I was only now—a decade later—telling my tale; to a complete stranger in a bar in the middle of nowhere, no less.

So what if she thought I was a perverted freak. I'd never have to see her again after tonight. My heart pounded in my chest. Maybe it was all the beer, but I felt suddenly liberated. Like ten years worth of shame was crumbling off my back all at once.

"Oh my god, there's *more*?" Maggie asked, giggling. Her eyes were laser focused on mine. She didn't seem the least bit phased by the first part. "Did you tell her you wanted to *fuck* her with that horrid thing? CAN you fuck with a rope-tied dick??"

This only encouraged me to continue my shameful story.

"Worse," I said, grinning like I was about to tell the punchline to a great joke. "My producer and I had a mutual friend we'd graduated college with. He played basketball for the school. He was almost seven foot tall and... black."

"Ok," Maggie said. "So what?"

"So, he also had a lot of really tall black friends. We'd recruited them to play the Deep Ones in our movie. They looked fucking great in their costumes. They towered above everyone, and since they were in giant monster suits, they only had to act with their bodies."

She nodded, not seeming to catch on to where the story was going. So I kept going.

"There were eight guys in all staying in two double-wide trailers across the lot from me and Julia, the girl in question. In the emails, I told her I wanted her to suck all eight big black dicks at once while I watched with my cock all knotted up so I couldn't jack off."

"Holy shit, you fucking pervert!" Maggie said, maybe only half-jokingly.

"Then I said I wanted to lick her pussy while they took turns fucking her in the ass."

"Would you still be wearing the cock knot at this point, or would you be free to jack off? What what would the other seven guys be doing while their friend was balls deep in her asshole?"

I laughed. Maggie hadn't missed a beat. She was into my insane story. She wasn't judging me at all, but rather trying to work out the logistics of the cuckold gangbang I'd just described.

"You're something else, you know that?" I said, smirking.

"*You're* something else, you big ole pervert!"

We just looked at each other smiling for a few moments. And then...

Maggie leaned in so close I thought she was going to kiss me. I could smell the beer on her breath. "So you like to watch, Brian Sully?"

"Depends," I said, feeling my loins stir from her closeness. "What am I gonna see?"

"Me." She leaped out of the booth and made a big production out of walking to the dance floor, hips swinging side to side, taking full advantage of her form-fitting dress.

An awful, twangy tune started playing on the jukebox, inspiring a whole slew of the rednecks playing pool, darts or just sitting around the tables to get up and join Maggie on the dance floor (including the old man she'd blown off to drink with me). She never took her eyes off of me as a potbellied, bearded guy in a cowboy hat danced up to her and put his hands on her hips from behind. She let him pull her ass up against his crotch and swayed with the shitty country tune, grinning wide the whole time.

I was erect under the table. Watching the fat dirtbag run his hands up and down Maggie's hips was driving me crazy, and she knew it. She grabbed his chubby hands and ran them up her shirt, letting go just before she got to her breasts. He copped a feel anyway, causing her to stick her tongue out at me.

When the awful song finished, she winked at me

and turned around, whispering something in his ear. When she was finished talking, she licked him on the cheek and kissed the spot. His face suddenly went from smirking to dead serious. He stopped dancing, tipped his hat, and left the dance floor. He walked right past the table full of his friends hooting and hollering at him for scoring such a gorgeous chick on the dance floor. Passing the tables, he reached the door, opened it, and left, causing his friends to break into confused murmuring.

Maggie rejoined me at the table, sliding in until her hips mashed up against my leg.

"What's up with him?" I asked, doing my best to mentally calm my erection.

"Somebody got hungry," she said, tipping back her beer.

"I thought you said you hated country music."

"I didn't say anything about country boys."

"Gross," I said, shaking my head in mock disgust.

"Your big head says no, but your little head..."

As she leaned her head back, downing the rest of her beer, she dropped the shoe off of her foot and rubbed my hard dick through my pants.

Our waitress stopped just then to drop off our new beers.

"He's got a boner," Maggie mock-whispered, pointing at the table. The waitress snorted, shook her head and walked away.

That's the moment I fell in love with Maggie the farm girl.

CHAPTER 6
THE FARM

I climbed back into my mother's car and crossed Phillips Family Farm off the list. I cranked the AC. Sweat rolled down my back. The summer sun was wreaking havoc on the black interior, causing the backs of my arms to stick against the hot leather.

Only four more to go.

I'd driven a total of 675 miles over five days.

Each time I arrived at the next farm, my heart would pound. Not because I was about to lie to a stranger about being lost out on his country road, but because I knew that sooner or later, I'd find the right farm.

That I would find Maggie.

It was only thirty miles to the next farm. The problem was, I was nearly out of gas, and stuck somewhere in the back roads of Indiana. I could backtrack out of there and lose the light of day, start again tomorrow, or hope that there was a small town with a gas station somewhere along this road in the next thirty miles and cover one more farm today.

I decided to take the chance.

There was no town.

My car died fifteen miles from the next farm. It was called simply LHS Farms. No listed phone number.

I turned on my flashers and locked my doors. I took off my shirt, wrapped it over my head desert-style, and started jogging down the winding road. It was already late afternoon when my GPS told me, *"Your destination is on the right."*

Even on foot, the gravel path was hard to find. There was no mailbox, and the foliage on both sides of the road had crept in over the narrow driveway. I unwrapped my head and wiped my face with my soaked shirt. My head throbbed from the heat. I recalled reading somewhere that one sign of heat stroke was when your body stopped sweating. My face was dry.

As I wound around the long, skinny road, it occurred to me that this farm could very well be abandoned. That I might find an old empty house with no electricity and no running water. I pictured myself calling Barry, begging him to drive to this middle-of-nowhere back road in central Indiana to pick me up.

If it comes to that, it comes to that, I thought. *She's worth it.*

At last, I rounded the final bend. The dense branches and bushes opened up, revealing an expansive landscape. Not as large as some of the farms I'd visited on my journey, but big enough to contain a two-story farmhouse situated in the middle of the property, a greenhouse nearly as tall and twice as long on the easternmost portion, and a small, rickety barn at the westernmost point. Behind the house, to the east, the earth was tilled, full of all sorts of vegetation that stretched all the way behind the greenhouse.

Inside the open barn door, I could see a pen with four or five goats rummaging through and eating from a thick stack of hay. A chicken coop rested against the barn, facing the house, its occupants clucking and dancing, making a general fuss of prancing around picking through the dirt for food.

Behind the barn, far enough back from the barn that I could see it from my vantage point at the front of the property, was a pigpen with plump swine rooting through mud, oinking and carrying on.

A filthy, rusted blue pickup truck sat at the end of the drive, close to the front porch of the old house. An old blue tarp tied to its rails covered the contents of its extended cab.

This farm was definitely not deserted.

I stumbled past the treeline, feeling lightheaded and sick to my stomach. Whoever lived here was going to have to let me rest for a while. Hopefully they'd be hospitable enough to drive me to the nearest gas station for fuel, then to my car. I didn't think I could walk another block in the heat, let alone fifteen more miles back to where I'd started.

I ascended the creaky steps of the house, noticing at once a musky, earthy smell, evidenced by the long rows of hanging flowerpots on either side of the paint-peeled door. I raised my hand to knock.

"Brian?"

I turned around, head throbbing, dazed. My mouth was so dry I felt my lips crack when they turned up in a huge smile.

Maggie.

She wore a slinky faux-fur leopard print bikini top and a pair of short brown shorts. Her hands were sheathed in thick gloves. She held garden sheers in one hand and a tuft of weeds in the other. Her face and arms were dirty and wet with sweat. Her thick hair was pulled back and tucked under a baseball cap.

She was more beautiful that way than she was all made up that night we'd spent together.

"You have to leave, right now."

My smile faded. The pounding in my head did not.

"I had to see you."

"You saw me, now leave." Her face was dead serious. She dropped the sheers and weeds, took off her gloves and met me on the porch. She hooked her arm under mine and pulled. "Where did you park?"

"I ran out of gas. I feel sick." I stumbled down the last few stairs and retched in the yard. Thick bile escaped my lips. Hot and sticky.

"Let me get my keys, I'll drive you to town." She turned to walk up the steps.

I fell down. "I—" I retched again. "I found you. I win. Where's my cookie?"

I blacked out.

I dreamed of green things.

I was laying in a bed in an upstairs room in the farmhouse. It was night. Hot. The windows were open. A breeze blew across my body. I was naked. I raised my head, looking down my torso at my erection. I felt drunk. No, drugged. Groggy. Was this a dream?

The room swayed back and forth. The walls looked as if they were squirming. When I looked closer, I saw why.

Small tendrils broke through the wood paneling all across the walls, wiggling back and forth. I swear the tendrils had voices like small children, all speaking at once. Too many voices to make out their words.

The ceiling groaned. I gazed up. A dark spot appeared. It grew outward like mold. forming the shape of a woman. The woman-shape expanded, descending slowly from the ceiling. Arms grew from the mass. Legs,hair. Tits. A face.

Two sun-yellow circles appeared, burning bright in its head. Eyes.

A slit opened—its mouth—revealing more tendrils inside.

The shape landed on me. Gently. Light as a feather. It felt like moss. Like a light sponge, cool against my sweaty skin. It lowered its head and whispered in my ear. Horrible words. Words I did not want to hear, but forgot as soon as it finished speaking them.

It rose back into the air. Hovering. Staring at me, hair writhing against the ceiling. It opened its legs. A single tendril emerged and descended from the smooth mound of its crotch. I lay there, my limbs too heavy to move, as the tendril wound its way around my dick, spiraling down all the way to my balls, then pulling taught.

The winding limb tugged gently on my erection, twisting back and forth, up and down. The sensation was like nothing I'd ever felt. Like being jacked off by lavender. Sucked on by clouds.

It took no time before I felt an orgasm growing in my balls. My scrotum tightened.

I cried out as my cock spurted, shooting milky cum all over my stomach. More cum than I could recall ever ejaculating before.

As I drifted back to sleep, the tip of the tendril opened up into a small mouth and sucked up all the cum as the moss woman above me smiled.

CHAPTER 7
SIZZLE SLICE

After one last round, we left the bar looking for food. It was safe to say I was lit up like a Christmas tree, teetering on wasted. Maggie strangely seemed mostly sober, even though she'd matched me shot for shot, beer for beer since we'd met.

"What time is it?" I asked as we strolled down the strip, further away from the convention hotel, toward a cluster of restaurants, gas stations and liquor stores.

"Time to get some food in this belly," she said, grabbing my hand, swinging it back and forth.

"What's good around here?" I asked, wondering how much longer I was going to be able to keep up with the younger woman. I wasn't twenty-five anymore—my all-night bender years were long behind me. After that much alcohol, I was usually lucky to get a microwaved hot pocket in me before passing out.

She looked at me, confused. "I don't live around here."

"Wait, you're not from Cincinnati?"

"Nope."

"Then what are you doing here?"

"Hanging out."

"Where are you from?"

"Around."

"Is your farm in Ohio?"

"PIZZA!" Maggie let go of my hand and broke away in a trot toward the building directly ahead. A big, gaudy neon sign displayed a giant slice of pizza and words that blinked on and off. *Sizzle Slice. Sizzle Slice. Sizzle Slice.*

By the time I got through the door, Maggie was already at the counter bouncing to some punk rock band blaring over the speakers. The place was cool. Way better than the country bar.

Their pizzas were pre-cooked and displayed in a glass case next to the counter. Each pizza had a ridiculous name and weird ingredients.

"The Return of the Wu." Maggie was leaning down in front of me, reading the titles, her shoulder brushing against my crotch.

I got hard again. Can a person die from too many erections?

"What's a Wu?" She turned, her face even with the bulge in my pants. She looked at it and grinned. She made a playful biting motion then stood up.

"Looks like ranch dressing, jalapenos, pepperoni and green peppers."

She rolled her eyes, "I know what's on it. I can read! But what the hell is a Wu?"

"You're Wu-ing me right now with those gorgeous fucking eyes," I said, pretending to grip my heart.

She made a gagging motion, pointing her finger at her mouth.

"You lovebirds ready to order?"

The pizza girls were both pretty—not Maggie pretty, but easy to look at. The cook had brown spiky hair and wore some metal band t-shirt. Her arms and chest were covered in cool tattoos of horror movie icons, monsters and music logos.

The counter girl, the one taking our order, she was the real looker. Her black hair was shaved on the sides, and her stretched earlobes contained huge clear plugs full of what looked like blood. Her eyebrows were tiny pencil streaks only traversing halfway across her brow, giving her a distinctly sinister look. Her demeanor, on the other hand, couldn't have been nicer. She smiled as we giggled and tried to pronounce the weird names of the pizzas.

When it was time to cash out, she just smiled and handed us our receipt with the order number on it.

Maggie took my hand and rushed us over to a booth. We were the only customers this late at night, so we had our pick of the seating. "She didn't charge us!" she half-whispered, leaning across the table so the girl couldn't hear us.

"She thinks you're hot," I said, staring deep into her eyes. "So do I."

"Laying it on thick, aren't we, Brian Sully?" She looked away, pretending that she was losing interest.

I loved the way she kept using my full name. Like I was someone important, yet she had no idea who I was in my professional career. I wasn't a rock star to her like I was to everyone else. I was just Brian Sully, some dude she picked up at a bar.

"You're the first person in a long time to make me feel like my life is worth more than just the movies I make. My identity is still wrapped up in that shit. Even after a decade of retirement, I'm still Brian Sully, film director. Even if the word disgraced is printed before my title now. Those will be the first words of my obituary. But you? You make me feel like a human being."

The cook girl set our pizza slices on the table, but she didn't leave.

I smiled up at her.

"Um, I hate to do this to you while you're eating, but..."

She pulled a DVD of *Sons of Dagon* out of her apron. "I had to work a double and didn't get to come to the convention today. My boyfriend and I LOVE your movies. So does Becca," she motioned to the counter girl who hid her face when we turned to look at her, "but she's too shy to say anything. Would you mind signing this for Sissy and Killa Freak?"

Once she was gone, Maggie said in a low, goofy voice, "For Sissy and Killa Freak!"

"I told you," I said, putting my hands behind my head with a mock smug look on my face. "Didn't I tell you?"

"Yeah, well," Maggie said in a playful tone, loading her pizza with red pepper flakes, "your movies probably suck." She stuck her tongue out at me before shoving the pizza in her mouth.

"You probably suck better."

She nearly spit her food out laughing at my lame joke.

We gobbled up our slices, continuing to mock one another, when some heavy metal song started playing over the speakers.

Maggie's eyes grew wide. "Oh my god, I love this song!"

"Is that Cookie Monster on vocals?" I asked, smirking at her.

She stuck her tongue out at me again. It was long and thick and I couldn't help imagining what it would feel like licking my balls. "Embrace the grind," she said, leaping up from the booth. She ran out to the middle of the lobby and started thrash dancing to the music. Becca the counter girl laughed and joined her, glancing over her shoulder at me to make sure I was watching. The girls wanted to put on a show for me.

Maggie obliged, letting the goth girl in close as the two of them headbanged and bounced up and down. Sissy wore tight black pants with a studded leather belt and platform shoes. Her tits were big and contained precariously inside a low-cut spaghetti strapped top.

Maggie took full advantage of this fact by openly groping her while mouthing *"Oh my god!"* to me, pointing at the busty girl's tits with her free hand. Sissy hooted from behind the counter, egging the two beauties on.

I got up and joined Sissy at the counter, making sure I had the best view in the house. As the girls grinded against each other, Sissy turned the music up, causing the girls to increase their tempo and force as they molested one another for our benefit.

That's when it happened.

While Maggie was watching for my reaction, Becca leaned in and kissed her on the mouth, then shoved her tongue inside. Maggie flinched, yanking her head back, her expression turning quickly to shock. Becca's arms dropped to their sides. Without hesitation, she turned toward the door and walked outside.

"Hey, wait a minute! Our shift isn't over yet!" Sissy yelled, rushing out from behind the counter. "I'm not cleaning this whole place by myself!"

She ran out the door, chasing after her co-worker, leaving Maggie and I alone in the lobby.

I turned down the metal music and joined my lovely companion.

She was noticeably shaken.

"What's the matter, don't like kissing pretty girls?"

She didn't crack a smile. Her face was pale white.

"Maybe you like kissing boys more." I couldn't help it. That might not have been the best time to kiss her, but I'd been waiting all night and the goth girl getting first dibs had—I hate to admit—made me a little jealous. So I went in for a kiss of my own.

"Brian, don't-"

But it was too late. I'd grabbed a handful of her red tresses and pulled her close, locking her lips with my own. After a second, she relaxed, allowing her tongue to explore mine, then she broke free.

A look of weird surprise had crossed her face. Her mouth was turned up in an odd smile.

"What the hell are you staring at, kid? Do I have pizza in my beard?"

She lunged forward and attacked my mouth with hers, shoving her tongue inside as far as it would go, then yanking it out. She sucked on lips, grinding her thigh into my throbbing cock.

"How?" she asked through sloppy wet kisses.

I knew I was a decent kisser, but I hadn't made out like this since college. I didn't know what had gotten into her all of a sudden, but I wasn't complaining. I groped her tits and pushed my dick against her so hard I thought I was going to give myself friction burn through my pants.

The door slammed. Sissy had returned. Becca had not.

"Hey, what the fuck did you say to her, man? She wouldn't talk to me, wouldn't even look at me. She just got in her car and drove away. Crazy chick almost took out another car in the parking lot!"

Maggie grabbed my hand and pushed passed Becca, dragging me out the door.

"Sorry! Thanks for the pizza!" I managed to get out before the door shut behind us.

Maggie attacked me again against the outside wall, planting kiss after kiss after kiss on me. My mouth was already getting sore from overuse.

"What's got you so excited all of a sudden?"

Maggie broke away, smirking, and walked backward, reaching into the back of her dress. "Shut up and take me back to your room." She fished out her bra and threw it at me, then took off running back toward my hotel.

After what happened with Becca, I should have

guessed. I should have known then; after all the time I'd spent with them in my imagination, all the time I spent crafting them for the big screen, I should have figured it out, but I was drunk and I lonely and I was horny.

I should have figured out that Maggie wasn't just randomly hanging out in Cincinnati. She wasn't a normal person.

She wasn't a person at all. Maggie was a monster.

CHAPTER 8
LUKE

I woke in a bed. A cold washcloth lay across my face. I pulled it away and assessed my surroundings. It was morning. Bright light invaded the bedroom—the same room from my dream.

I pulled the sheet away. I was fully clothed. I felt a strange sense of relief. The musky smell of the old house, the weird way Maggie acted when I showed up—I was psyching myself out. My overactive imagination had me spooked.

At least I didn't really get jacked off by a moss woman's tentacle-dick, I thought, climbing out of bed.

The throbbing in my head started again and I had to sit back down. The sun must have really fucked me up. I noticed for the first time a fresh glass of water on the nightstand to my right.

Maggie must have gotten me up here and put me to bed the evening before. Left me the water.

I drank deeply from the glass and stayed seated like that, holding my head in my free hand, wondering if I should have just gone back to the coast after the film fest, when I heard muffled shouting from a room down the hall.

I rose slowly, making sure I wouldn't pass out and dream of fucking vegetation again. When I was sure I would remain conscious, I stepped lightly out into the hallway. The musky stench grew sharper and more pronounced out here.

The stairs were to my right; to my left were two additional bedrooms. I walked as quietly as the creaky hardwood floors would allow toward the sound of the muffled voice.

"No I will not!"

Maggie's voice.

I heard nothing in return.

"He's different, Mother. He's not like the rest of them."

Shit. The mother. A wave of guilt came over me. I shouldn't have barged into Maggie's life like this. I should have let it be a one night stand—the best one night stand of my life, but a one night stand nonetheless. I was making family trouble for her.

I decided to leave. I'd get a few blocks down the road from Maggie's farm and then call Barry to come pick me up. It'd take him three hours if he left the second I called, but I figured I could manage the heat this time by sneaking some waters out of the fridge. I'd leave a few twenties on the table, and sit in the shade of some trees on the side of the road and wait. Fuck being here messing with Maggie's life any longer.

I turned to go and stopped dead in my tracks.

In front of me stood a huge figure, silent, staring.

"Not supposed to be here."

It was a man—at least his features were that of a man in his thirties, but his demeanor and childlike speech betrayed a mental handicap. He stood awkwardly with his arms crossed in front of his dirty overalls and long-sleeved plaid shirt. He wore thick gloves similar to those Maggie had worn. He stood at least six-five, but from my perspective looking up at him, he seemed even bigger, like a giant.

"You belong in the garden."

"Do I?" Speaking made me wince. My headache seemed to have only gotten worse.

The door slammed behind me.

"Leave him alone, Luke." Maggie still wore her little bikini top from the day before, but she'd lost the hat. Her hair fell across her shoulders and back, licking the tops of her breasts like flames.

"He belongs in the garden. Yes he does."

"Sorry about him," Maggie said, pushing past me, toward the lumbering oaf. "Go find something to do. Feed the goats."

"Already fed 'em."

"Feed them again!"

Luke flinched at Maggie's raised voice. Sulking, he walked slowly toward the stairs, adding as he clomped down them, "...Belongs in the garden."

"That your boyfriend?"

Maggie laughed, but it seemed forced. Not the joyful, playful laugh from before. From our night together.

Below us, the front door slammed. She motioned for me to follow and we descended the stairs, entering the living room.

I took a chair. She sat down on the couch across from me. "Luke's my brother. He's... slow. But he's a hard worker. This farm wouldn't function without him."

"Seems like a nice guy." I raised my eyebrows as I drank from my glass.

There was anxiety behind Maggie's eyes. Something was off. I shouldn't have come; I was sure of that now. This whole nonsense had been a silly mistake, my judgment clouded by romantic notions and dramatics.

"You gonna stare at me all day? I know I'm pretty, but..."

"Why'd you come here, Brian?"

"Getting right to the point. Alright. I had to see you again. The way you left, I just... This thing. Us. It seemed unfinished. I had to see it through. I had to find you."

She just stared, hands in her lap.

"I told you I would. You still haven't given me my cookie."

"I thought you were joking. Just being a cheese-ball, trying to get in my pants."

"I can leave."

"You should."

"Show me the place first? I drove a long way to see you. Car's out of gas. It'll take my ride at least a few hours to get here."

Maggie sighed, annoyed. "There's a gas can in the back of the truck. I'll drive you out." She stood up. "How the fuck did you find me, anyway?"

"Luck?"

"No such thing."

"Would you think I was a weirdo if I told you I searched the internet for every independently owned farm anywhere slightly near Cincinnati, Ohio?"

"You're in my house, Brian. You are fucking weird."

"Touché."

"Come on. Let me show you my shit. Then you have to leave."

"Hang on," I said. "Before you throw me out, can I at least say what I came all the way out here to say?"

Maggie looked at me—Annoyed? Impatient? Why was she in such a hurry to throw me out of her house? The place was clean enough, if a little weird smelling. There didn't seem to be a whole lot to do today (not that I knew anything about farming).

"Well?" she said, finally. She eased back down onto the couch. "Say your shit."

I looked into my nearly empty glass, suddenly embarrassed, the full weight of the awkward meeting hitting me all at once. I was a completely insane person. A one night stand who somehow managed to stalk my way back into this woman's life. She was just being polite to get me to leave without axe-murdering her whole family or something. Any minute now she was going to excuse herself to call the cops and have me thrown off her property.

"It's... I-"

"Oh for fuck's sake, Brian Sully. You didn't track me to the ends of the Earth to get the fear right at the moment of truth. Man up, you fucking pussy!"

She was busting my balls. There it was. All the reassurance I needed. I took a deep breath and smiled. "Let's talk about it while we walk."

***

As we walked west toward the barn, I reached out and tried to take Maggie's hand.

She pulled away.

"I'm sorry I ruined your life."

Maggie glanced back at me, frowning. "No, Brian. It's just... I... It's really complicated. I should have never spent that night with you. It-"

"Was a mistake?"

We were at the pigpen.

Sadness filled Maggie's eyes. She didn't speak, didn't deny what I'd said.

"Your husband isn't going to come trucking up that gravel drive any minute, is he?"

"I'm not married."

"Boyfriend?"

"No. These are the pigs."

"I see that. They look like they'll make mighty fine bacon."

She showed me the goats, the chickens, and a small

pond that had been hidden from my view upon arrival containing several types of fish.

"That's the grand tour," she said as we circled our way back toward the truck.

As much as I knew I should leave, I couldn't bring myself to say it. Being near Maggie again—even weird Maggie—made my heart ache. It was absurd that someone I'd only spent one night with could make me feel emotions this strong. I searched for any excuse I could to stay.

"You didn't show me the garden or the greenhouse. Can I see the garden?"

"It's a garden."

"Are there flowers?"

"Yes."

"What kind?"

"Roses."

"Let's go see roses."

"I'd rather show you the greenhouse."

"What's in the greenhouse?"

"Green things. None of this stuff is very interesting. It's just a little farm. We really should go, befor-"

I pulled her close, kissing her mouth.

She didn't return it, instead letting her face go limp.

I leaned back, still gripping her around the waist. "I needed this, goddamn it. Even if you didn't. I'm glad I came out here and found you, otherwise I would have spent the rest of my life wondering 'what if?' 'What if she was *the one* everyone talks about?' What if I'd found the girl of my dreams and she'd run off in the dead of night, never to be seen or heard from again? I'll never come back. Never bother you again. I-"

She leaned in and kissed me, hard and full. When she pulled away, she had tears streaming down her face.

I smirked. "Does this mean I get to see the greenhouse?"

***

It was even hotter inside the greenhouse than it was outside. The heat lamps burned on either side of the huge room, beating down on the multitude of different types of plant life. The humidity was so high, rivulets of condensation rolled down the plastic walls.

"You could grow some great fucking weed in here," I said, picking a row to walk down.

"Who says I'm not?"

"You holding out on me, Maggie?"

Still no laughter. Not even a giggle.

There were rows and rows of multicolored peppers, leafy greens, tomato plants, green beans, cucumbers and many other vegetable-like things. We rounded the corner at the end of the greenhouse without saying anything and headed back up toward the front.

She was rushing me. I had to buy more time. I felt like the world was spinning in fast-motion. Some part of me thought I'd never see her again, that my crazy trip through the Midwest visiting farm after farm would end without ever turning up my girl.

I suppose a part of me *wanted* that to happen. Wanted to be able to go back to the coast, back to my shitty novels and the grocery store, satisfied that I'd done everything in my power to find her.

But here I was. And she was trying to get rid of me as fast as she could.

"Whoa!" I said, eyeing a row of Venus flytraps, pitcher plants, little spiky-leafed plants called sundews, bladderworts, and various other carnivorous species.

"Ah, yes. Our meat-eaters."

"It won't shock you to learn this, Maggie, but I was a weird child. I was obsessed with carnivorous plants. I used to collect these things when I was a kid. I'd drop ants, beetles, spiders, any little living thing I could find in these things and watch them munch! Feed me, Seymour!"

73

I said, pretending to drip blood over the mouth of a flytrap.

"I wouldn't do that. Might take off your hand," Maggie said, finally smirking for the first time today.

I was getting to her, breaking down this weird defensive shell she'd had since I got here. Good. This trip might turn out OK after all...

We got back to the front of the greenhouse. I spun around to face her. "I need your phone number, or at least let me give you mine. My mother only lives a few hours from here. When I'm in town, I'm relatively close. I won't come back here, but—"

The doors crashed open. Luke was back.

"Mother says she wasn't finished talking to you. Mother says to come back to her. Now."

Was that panic on Maggie's face?

"I have to take Brian to his car, I'll—"

The hulking figure grabbed her by the arm with one of those thick brown gloves, and flung her down to the dirt. "Go to mother!"

"Hey, listen!" I yelled, stepping up to larger man.

I wasn't big, nor was I any kind of fighter, but I wasn't about to watch Maggie get manhandled. I didn't give a fuck if the dude was her brother or not. Didn't give a fuck how big he was, either.

I shoved at him with both arms. He didn't budge.

With one swift move, he backhanded me. It felt like I'd been hit with a tree trunk. I crumpled to the floor next to Maggie.

"Brian!" Maggie jumped to her feet. She punched Luke in the chest. He didn't so much as flinch. "You fucking asshole!"

I got up as well. "I'm fine, I'm fine." I was lying. I couldn't catch my breath. My chest felt like a hole had been punched through it. "Listen. I know this is my fault. I didn't mean to cause a family squabble, but—"

Luke pulled his gloves tighter. "Mother wants him

in the garden."

"What's so important about the garden, bud?" I said, stilling catching my breath, trying my best to make it seem like I wasn't shitting-my-pants scared. I was failing.

"Food grows in the garden."

Maggie's eyes were wide with fear. She stood between Luke and I, acting as a barrier. She spoke quickly, loudly, deliberately. "If you want to live, you have to run. Right now. Run for your fucking life!"

CHAPTER 9
THE HOTEL ROOM

I swiped the card key through the door and opened it. Maggie walked inside, letting her hand brush across my crotch on the way in. I grinned. I couldn't help but think again about the night I stood in the water on the coast. To think I'd hesitated to come back out on the road.

I let the door shut behind me. "Should we rent some movies on the TV, or...?"

"Shut up and kiss me." Maggie pushed me down on the bed and dove on top of me, smothering me with another round of wet, sloppy kisses.

I hitched up her flower dress and squeezed her ass, causing her to groan, low and guttural.

She shifted her weight to the left, sliding off of me, running her hand down my chest and belly until it rested on the bulge in my pants. She squeezed it with the same urgency as I was still squeezing her ass. She fumbled with my belt, button and zipper, then yanked down my pants.

She shifted position again, finally breaking her mouth away from mine. She curled her body around my chest, then with both hands, pulled my boxer briefs down around my balls, freeing my erection.

"I haven't ever done this before. Be gentle with me," I said in a mockingly high voice.

"Shut up." She giggled, facing me again, kissing me anew while sliding her ice-cold fingers around my warm shaft for the first time.

She wrenched up my shirt, pecked me on the mouth several more times, then lowered her head to my right nipple. She licked and teased the sensitive area with her teeth while she jacked me off. Her free hand came up across my chest, pinching and rolling my left nipple.

I moaned loudly, dropping my head against the pillow. The combination of alcohol, pizza and exhaustion from my long day of signing autographs and talking to fans was finally beginning to take its toll. I was fighting sleep even with the absolute expert way in which Maggie manipulated my body. I felt like I was in some kind of bizarre sex trance. I was so out if it, I could swear for a moment, when I opened my eyes, that Maggie's hair was moving of its own volition, slithering and swaying to the rhythm of her handjob and nipple tweaks.

That's when I tried to put my hand inside her panties.

She let go of my cock and rolled across my body, yelping as she did so.

I held my hands back to show I was not a threat. "Not a rapist. I swear. You OK?"

"Sorry," she said, settling down. She slid across my chest and pecked me on my mouth, laying her head on my shoulder. "I'm on my period. You almost made a mess."

"Yeah, sure," I said, pulling away and laying her head gently on the pillow as I raised up onto my elbow. "'Cause I've never heard that one before."

She barked a short laugh. "You think I'm lying?" She raised up to her knees and started to tug off her panties. "You want me to sit on your face to prove it?"

I didn't say anything.

She giggled. "Well do you?"

"You don't see me saying no." I smirked and raised my eyebrows.

"Sick! You're a sick freak!" she said, collapsing onto me, dropping half a dozen kisses on my bare chest as she pushed me down onto my back.

"The story about the black man gangbang didn't phase you, but red wings is where you draw the line? Noted."

"Shut the fuck up," she said, tweaking my bare nipple.

I yelped and covered myself for protection. "I probably have a deck of cards down in the rental car," I said, resting my hands behind my head. "Or we could ask room service to send us up a chess board. I'd whip your ass at chess."

As a response, she reached down and pulled her flower dress over her head in one motion, exposing her breasts to me for the first time. "Or you could shut the fuck up and let me suck your dick."

"Not until I get to do some sucking of my own!" I grabbed her and flung her to the bed. Her breasts were full, but not big. They were firm, only falling to the sides of her chest ever so slightly when she was on her back. The nipples stuck up and out at that perfect angle. The mere sight of them causing my erection to take on a density not felt since my horny high school years.

I kissed her mouth deeply, then pulled away and kissed her lightly on the nose, on her cheek, on her ear, causing her to writhe beneath me. I kissed her neck. She dug her nails into my back. I kissed her collar bone, then her chest, then finally I chose a course down her left breast, dropping a line of smooches as I went. I cupped it with my right hand and kissed the nipple, lightly. Then I danced a circle around its puffy light pink areola with my tongue, resting finally in the center of her nipple, latching on with my mouth. I returned the favor she'd given me by reaching up with my left hand and tweaking her left nipple while I licked and sucked the right one.

She moaned and squealed, wrapping both her legs around my right leg and dry humping against my exposed dick so hard I actually felt the beginning tingles of an orgasm begin to brew, causing me to break away so that I didn't embarrass myself by splooging all over her stomach just from sucking on her tits.

"Ok, you can blow me now," I said, making a big production out of flopping back onto the bed, hands clasped across my chest, big shit-eating grin on my face.

She laughed and punched me lightly in the stomach, which I overplayed, acting as if I'd been shot.

"You're such a dork!" she said, nearly snorting.

"Takes one to know one."

She slid down my body. Her naked breasts felt like warm clouds against my bare skin. She took my hard-on back into her hand and stroked, slowly. She flicked her tongue out, getting the tip wet, never breaking eye contact with me.

"Don't suck it too good, now. You'll make me fall in love, then you'll have to take me home to meet your Momma."

She choked back a laugh. "Yeah, that's not gonna happen. My mother is... let's just say she's peculiar."

I rose up on my elbows. The grin left my face. "Do you hang out in Cincinnati often? If I come back here, will I see you again?"

Her expression became serious as well, although she continued to lightly stroke my erection, dropping little kisses on its head between words as she spoke. "I don't know. It's a possibility. I'm not really sure how long I'm gonna stick around after this season. There's... a lot of work to do on the farm."

"Can I come see you on the farm? Where is it?"

"That's... That's not a good idea..."

"What if I can find it myself? What do I win?"

"A cookie?" she said halfheartedly. It was clear she didn't want to have this conversation.

An awkward silence broke out between us for the first time. Not thirty seconds had gone by all night long without one of us or the other saying something weird, making a snide comment or throwing back to some inside joke we'd told earlier in the night that only the two of us would understand.

"Fuck. I ruined it," I said, feeling like a complete idiot. I covered my face with my hands. "I'm sorry. I shouldn't have said that, it's just, I–"

Suddenly my cock was down her throat. I gasped and opened up my eyes. Her lips were touching the small tuft of pubic hair at the base of my penis. Her eyes were still locked with mine.

"Oh my fucking god," I moaned, collapsing back on the pillow.

We stayed like that for some time. She sucked me, licked and rubbed my balls, pumped my shaft up and down, switching hands when one got tired and rubbing my cock against one side of her face, then the other when her mouth got tired.

To say she knew how to suck a cock was an understatement. After a long while, we switched positions, her on her left side, me on my right, face-fucking her with both my hands wrapping her hair into knots, her hands guiding the depths of my thrusts, circling my shaft in front of her mouth, squeezing gently when I tried to plunge too far, momentarily blocking my entrance into her soft, warm throat.

We ended the session at the foot of the bed, her on her knees, me standing over her. She worked my shaft with her right hand, my balls with her left. Saliva dripped freely from my scrotum, her hands glistening fists full of slobber.

"I'm close," I said, hitching my breath. Smiling, I

said, "I probably shouldn't cum on your face the first night we met. Don't want you to think I'm a slut."

"You can cum on my face," she said between sucks. "Or my tits, or my stomach, or my ass."

She took her mouth away, increasing the speed of her hand against the head of my dick.

My knees went weak. She knew she had me at the brink of orgasm.

She slowed down, granting me momentary mercy.

"But if it was up to me," she said, taking my cock all the way down to the root again, sticking her tongue out to lick my balls for good measure, then extracting it from her throat just as fast. "I'd take your load down my throat."

That's all it took. I rocked my hips and let out several quick, grunting expletives as I grabbed the back of her head and forced my dick back down her throat.

Three long ejaculations went right into her belly. Then I was spent. I fell onto the bed, my calves on fire, my lower back screaming in pain. I took long, deep breaths as my pulse hammered in my ears. "Jesus, Marry and motherfuck," I said, wiping the sweat from my face. "No one's ever sucked my dick for two hours before."

Maggie laughed and crawled onto me, laying her head in the puddle of sweat pooling on my chest. "I like sucking your cock. You make a lot of noise."

"How could I not? You fucking sucked the life out of me."

She looked at me slyly. "Not quite. I bet there's a little more soul in there. Let's find out."

She went for my dick again. I had to grab her head and stop her. "No, no, no. Fucking hell. I'm an old man, not a sixteen year old kid. Give me a few minutes first, Christ almighty."

She flopped back onto me. "You're a cool dude, Brian Sully."

There was the full name again. I brushed her hair

out of her face and just gazed at her. She glowed from exertion. Her cheeks were red from cock burn, her lips swollen even bigger than normal from sucking (which was saying something, considering their regular puffiness).

Finally I asked, "What's your favorite part of the farm? You told me about the animals, the hard work. But out of everything you do there everyday, what's the thing you like the most about it?"

She considered my question for a long while, tracing lines in my belly hair, twirling it up on her fingers, then letting it spring back down into wet curly Q's. "Honestly?" she asked, returning my gaze. "The trees. The trees are my favorite part."

"Trees? Trees are everywhere. What's so special about the trees on your farm?"

"Not just the trees on my farm. All trees. Trees are free."

"How are trees free? They never move."

"The seeds. They blow away. They travel with the winds, get picked up by birds or little animals. They end up far, far away from where they started. Then they put down roots and start anew. They make a home in a faraway land, and the cycle starts all over again."

I didn't say anything. Just gawked at her.

She laughed and put her hand on her face, groaning. "That was a stupid answer, huh? I should have said the pigs."

"That was the most perfect answer to any question I've ever heard answered in the history of questions." I said, causing her to slap my bare chest.

"Shut the fuck up!"

"I'm serious," I said, giggling. Then the smile left my face. I lifted her off me and sat up, crossing my legs.

She did the same.

I cleared my throat and wiped the sweat and laughter-tears from my eyes, clearing them so I could see her perfectly while I said what I had to say next.

"Listen," I said, putting my hands on her shoulders so I had her full attention. "Aw fuck, this is embarrassing."

"Go ahead. Don't get all shy on me now. You just spunked down my throat. Your little swimmers are dying inside of me right now," she said, rubbing her stomach.

"Alright, fine." I locked eyes with her. "This might just be a normal date for you. Just a fun night with a decent enough dude, but... Shit. I have to be honest with you. I have to say this right now or I'll hate myself forever. No one has ever made me feel the way you've made me feel tonight—at least not since I've been an adult. Not since I've known what real love is."

I faltered for a moment, anxiety rising in my chest.

"I've only known you for one night, but—God damn it, I feel so fucking lame for saying this, but I fucking love you, Maggie." Tears welled up in my eyes. "I fucking know I do. I'm a forty-three year old man, not some fucking child. I know what puppy love is. I know this isn't that. I know what this is. This is real. I know I'm in fucking love with you."

Maggie just stared at me.

My heart pounded. I'd fucked the whole thing up with some dumb, desperate speech about love. This drop-dead sexy girl probably had three or four dates a week. How many of them ended just like this, with some lame old dude confessing his love for a girl fifteen years younger than him whose only intention was to have a fun night out and get laid? I'd ruined it for real.

"What if I'm not who you think I am?" she asked, finally.

"What? You're not funny, whip-smart, gentle, caring, considerate, and weird as shit?" My heart still hammered in my chest. She hadn't told me to go fuck myself yet. Was there still a chance to save this night?

She seemed to choose her next words carefully.

"What you said at the pizza place—about me making you feel human. You make me feel that way, too."

"Well that's not 'I love you too, Brian,' but I'll take it," I said, feeling the cold burn of rejection rise in my throat.

Then she jumped into my arms and nearly strangled me with a hug around my neck, squeezing all the air out of me. She whispered in my ear "I love you too, Brian."

We fell asleep just like that, her vice-grip around me, laying on our sides, softly crying into each other's skin, overwhelmed with emotion.

That night, I didn't dream.

***

When I woke up the next day, she was gone.

"Maggie?"

No response.

I cleared the beer and pizza phlegm from my throat and climbed out of bed. I felt surprisingly good for someone who'd just woken from his first all-night bender in years. I walked toward the bathroom, stretching out my arms and legs, loosening them up.

She wasn't in the bathroom.

Panic set in. She hadn't left me her phone number. I didn't even know her last name.

Maybe she went down to the lobby for breakfast. Stop being a spazz, I thought, grabbing my pants and shirt. I put my shoes on without socks and made my way to the door, almost forgetting my room key in my rush.

She wasn't in the dining room.

I saw Barry in the lobby as he was making his way toward the wing of the hotel that was hosting the final day of the film festival.

"You look like hell, bro! You get some last night?"

"No. Yes. Sort of. Look, Barry, I'm trying to find someone right now, can we talk later?"

Barry motioned toward his wrist, indicating time was short. He walked backwards down the hall. "Gotta be at our second screening by noon-thirty, Buddo. Don't be late! Your fans are waiting!"

I approached the front desk. "Did you see a red-haired woman come through the lobby this morning? Uh, green flower dress? Very pretty?"

The counter clerk was maybe nineteen. His pimpled face turned downward into a frown. "Can't say that I did, sir. But I've only been on duty for thirty minutes."

"Thanks anyway," I said, my heart sinking.

"Say, aren't you Brian Sully? My wife and I LOVE your movies! Could I get an autograph?"

***

I sulked through the rest of the festival, playing the previous night's events over and over in my head, trying to figure out what I'd done or said that made Maggie disappear on me like this. I don't remember introducing the second screening of *Sons of Dagon*. I don't remember the Q and A that followed, or the signing that afternoon. All I could think about was Maggie.

"I love you too, Brian."

Those words haunted me. Before Barry and I left the film festival, I canceled my flight back to Oregon. I called my mother and told her I'd be staying with her indefinitely.

I had to find her.

I had to be with Maggie.

CHAPTER 10
MOTHER

"I'm calling the fucking cops. This is crazy." I pulled out my cell phone and went to dial.

Luke surged forward and slapped the phone out of my hand. It landed in the dirt. He stepped on it with his huge brown boot, smashing it further into the earth. "You go in the garden now."

"Look, motherfucker," I said, still reeling from his first blow but full of enough adrenaline to fight off Luke's next swing. Or so I told myself. The truth was, I'd never been in a fistfight in my entire life. In fact, I'd been bullied relentlessly in my shitty small town junior high and high schools.

I didn't know how to throw a punch, let alone dodge one.

"Let him leave, Luke! Just let him leave!" Maggie pleaded, grabbing her brother's arm. "He doesn't know anything! He just wanted to see me!"

"What don't I know? What the fuck is going on on this farm that I don't know about?"

Luke ignored me, focusing instead on his sister. "Mother said."

"Mother said! Mother said! You know what, I'm gonna go talk to your fucking mother right now. Does she know how you treat Maggie out here?" I slipped past the two siblings and jogged out the door toward the big house.

"Brian!" Maggie called behind me. Her voice was frantic and full of fear.

But I'd already broken into a full run. Neither of them would catch up to me by the time I got in the house. I jumped up the porch steps three at a time and rushed through the front door, slamming and locking it behind me.

I didn't really know what the fuck I was doing, I was just going off of instinct. Luke had assaulted me and put his hands on Maggie. If I had to take her off this farm myself, that's exactly what I intended to do.

But first I had to meet this Mother. Had to see if there was a less dramatic way to end this awful disaster of a trip to Maggie's farm.

I climbed the stairs as Luke and Maggie got to the front door. They banged and yelled for a second, then got quiet. They'd get to the back door in a moment, but not soon enough. I'd already made it to their mother's room.

I knocked on the door. "Mrs. uh..." It occurred to me then that I still didn't know Maggie's last name. The address for the farm simply said LHS Farm. No name. "Miss, I need to talk to you." I knocked again. "My name is Brian, I'm a friend of Maggie's." Still no answer.

I tried the door. Locked.

"Miss? Hello?"

No response.

"Brian, stop!"

Maggie's voice. She and Luke had made it through the back door. What the hell was I doing? I didn't even know these people. I'd spent one night, one fucking night with Maggie. Now, there I was, banging on her mother's bedroom door in the middle of some crazy family drama.

A grown ass man. I was a crazy person. I'd lost my goddamn mind out there in Oregon with those mountain people.

I considered meeting them at the steps, letting Maggie drive me back to my car. But I didn't.

If I left now, if I let her drop me off at my car, I'd never see her again.

I let that sit. Thought about it. Decided then, in that moment, that I could not live without Maggie.

A calmness took over me.

It was as simple as that. Maggie was all that mattered.

I turned around and kicked the door in.

Nothing.

***

Inside the room there was nothing. No furniture. No bedding. No Mother. The floors and walls were completely bare. The stillness, in fact, was unsettling— how much nothing occupied that space. Maggie had stood in this empty room, behind the closed door, and had an argument with someone I couldn't hear. Had she been talking to herself?

Confused, I stepped further into the room. I heard Maggie and Luke ascend the steps and enter the doorway, but I didn't turn around. Instead I just stood there like an idiot, trying to make sense of the situation.

"You belong in the–"

"Fuck your garden," I said, facing them at last. "What's going on here? Where is she?"

"She's everywhere," Maggie said in a small voice, looking at the floor. "It wasn't too late. You could have gone."

"Does your mother even live here? Is she even alive?"

"Enough," Luke said, plodding forward.

The room was too small to get out of his way. I was trapped between the the far wall and the window that looked down onto the front yard. I backed up until my back pressed against the wall. "Get the fuck back!" I screamed.

Luke grabbed me around the throat and lifted me off the ground. My eyes bugged out as I grabbed his gloves, trying in vain to create air space so I could breathe. Fear overtook me and I flailed my legs as he turned around and began walking me toward the door. I kicked him in the chest and face.

He didn't so much as wince, even though my feet were leaving scuff marks on his cheeks.

Then I felt his glove come loose.

I reared back both my feet and kicked off his chest as hard as I could. I went crashing—one of Luke's gloves in hand—to the hardwood floor at Maggie's feet. What I saw next knocked the wind out of me harder than the fall.

The hand. Its fingers had actually been bent at a joint inside the glove. Free now, they unfurled. They looked more like a bundle of sticks than fingers, with long black spines at the tips that resembled a hornet's stinger, or an impossibly long barb from a rose bush.

The hand itself was greenish-brown and cracked. Pieces of it had already broken off and littered the floor at Luke's feet like dead leaves. The cracked flesh traveled up inside of his plaid jacket.

My mind tried to make sense of it. Tried to see it as another glove that had been inside the glove that I still held in my hand with a death grip. But that was crazy.

All of this was crazy.

And so I ran.

I grabbed Maggie by the arm and dashed through the door before Luke could get to us again. We took the stairs two at a time and rounded the bottom step before Luke had lumbered out of the empty room.

I flung the door open, never letting go of Maggie,

and ran to the truck as fast as my legs would allow.

I still hadn't made sense of what I'd seen. I kept saying, *"What the fuck? What the fuck? What the fuck?"* under my breath.

I wrenched the creaking, rusted driver's side door open and pushed Maggie in first. I climbed in behind her. The keys were in the ignition. I turned it over. It sputtered, but didn't start.

I turned it over again.

Luke appeared in the doorway. That hand. It was still the same. Still impossible.

I turned the key over a third time and the engine roared to life.

I slammed the gear shifter in reverse and floored it. But it was too late. Luke had cleared the stairs. He lifted his green arm high and smashed it down, tearing into the metal front end of the truck before the wheels had found traction to move us backward.

He lifted the front end into the air, preventing us from moving at all.

"What the fuck is that thing, Maggie?! *What the fuck is it?!*" I screamed frantically, my mind still refusing to accept the reality in front of me.

She just stared forward as if catatonic, a morose expression on her face.

I gripped the steering wheel tight and mashed the gas pedal anyway, as if somehow the tires would find traction in the air and move us to safety.

The the front end cracked and groaned. Suddenly we were back on the ground, flying backward across the yard. Luke was left standing in front of the house, holding the truck's front bumper. I howled with laughter, in total disbelief at our luck. I slammed on the brakes and shifted into drive, ready to pull a U-turn and drive the fuck out of there.

That's when Luke threw the bumper.

***

I dove over Maggie, pushing her down in the seat as the front windshield exploded in on us. The bumper missed my head by inches, bounced off the seat then back out onto the hood of the truck.

I sat up in disbelief. "He's trying to fucking kill us!"

Luke ran toward the truck.

Instinct kicked in. In my normal life, I was not an aggressive or angry person at all. I wouldn't even raise my voice to a shitty waitress who got my order wrong at a restaurant, or an annoying telemarketer that wouldn't take no for an answer.

But this wasn't my normal life. This was some bizarre world where I fell in love with mysterious farm girls and got attacked by their mutant brothers.

I slammed the gas. The force pushed the bumper off the side of the hood onto the ground. "Hold on, Maggie!"

The truck got to Luke before Luke got to us. I ran him clean over. The suspension groaned as the truck pitched up into the air and then slammed back down once we'd run him over. I hit the brakes and spun the wheel, cutting a sharp turn just in front of the porch, circling back around to face the downed farm boy.

Even after everything, I still couldn't believe what I saw next.

The plaid shirt had been torn away under the tires of the truck. His suspenders hung in ruins around his waist.

Luke was not human. Not anywhere close to it.

His torso was the same crumbling, greenish-brown texture that I'd first glimpsed on his hand and arm. Indeed, his entire body seemed to be nothing more than a jumbled collection of sticks, twigs, and roots with thick ivy running crisscross, holding the whole chaotic mess together into a man-shape. Only his head and neck were human; and now, without the shirt collar to cover it, I could see the places where the human flesh was rotting and peeling away.

He charged the truck again.

This time his cry was guttural, inhuman, no longer the child-like voice he used when he pretended to be a person.

I gritted my teeth and braced for impact as we closed in on him, but no impact came. Luke leaped clear over the car, landing behind us, in front of the house. That left our path to the gravel drive clear. I yipped with joy and slammed the gas. In just a moment, this nightmare would be over. We could drive straight to a police station and report—whatever it was that had just happened. I could take Maggie to safety. I could be with her.

Then, just as we got to speed, she reached over and, with one hand, ripped the steering wheel, gear shifter, and ignition system off the dash board with one single yank.

Maggie, a young woman of maybe a hundred and fifteen pounds, one-handed, demolished the interior of the truck faster than a grown man with a set of power tools would have been able to.

Impossible. The empty room. The monster brother. The super strong girl. This was all impossible.

The truck rolled to a stop. I stared forward, wide-eyed. Shock and disbelief had me frozen in place.

Maggie dropped the steering column out the window. "I'm sorry, Brian. She would have let you leave. She would have let you live."

CHAPTER 11
THE ROSE GARDEN

Luke caught up to the truck and wrenched me out with one of his humongous claws. I didn't fight back or so much as scream. Maggie had rendered the truck useless with just one of her little hands. The same hands she'd used on me when we made love. So gentle. So careful.

I watched her get out of the truck, a frown on her face, as Luke dragged me behind him. I lay there limp, not fighting back. I knew exactly where we were going.

He was taking me to the garden.

As he dragged me past the greenhouse to an isolated spot against the treeline that wasn't visible from the front yard, I stared at Maggie. Her hair was the same. Her face, her tits, her arms and legs. She looked exactly the same as the girl I'd fallen in love with. But the spark was gone. The mischievous spark she had in her eye the night we'd met—it was as though this farm had sucked the life out of her, dimmed her shine, kept her from being herself.

Even in that terrifying moment when I should have been struggling for my life—should have been wrenching against Luke's giant claw—I knew I loved her.

And more than I wanted to save myself, I wanted to save Maggie.

Luke dropped me. I turned to see the garden. To see the fucking roses.

The rose garden consisted of a single row of rosebushes twenty feet long across the perimeter of the treeline that separated the farm property from the small road at the head of the gravel drive. The soil in front of the bushes was freshly plowed and dark. It was thick and rich. Laying all across it, from one side to the other, front to back, were rose pedals. Pinks and reds of all different hues lay there, layer upon layer, creating one huge, magnificent bed of roses.

The pungent odor that permeated the farm—the smell that seemed so distinct at the greenhouse—emanated from this spot. From the rose garden. Now, here, in front of it, I could finally discern the smell. It was the unmistakable aroma of rotting corpses.

And what finally got my legs moving again, what finally broke that spell of numbness, what got me back on my feet trying to run away, was the freshly dug grave directly in front of me.

My grave.

"Maggie! Maggie, please!" The monster man and the impossibly strong woman didn't have to make sense. Didn't have to be logical for my basic survival instinct to reduce me to crying and begging. "Please don't do this to me! I'll leave! I'll go right now! I'll walk, just let me go!"

I tried to scurry in the opposite direction of the grave, snot and slobber falling out of my face, but Luke took one of his massive arms and plucked me off the ground, turning me back toward the rose garden.

And that's when things really got weird.

The surface of the bed of roses began to roil. The dank smell of rotting flesh became even stronger, if that was possible. And then, one by one, heads broke through the dark soil.

Human heads.

Or at least they had been human at some point. Now they were greens and browns, some cracked and flaking like Luke's monstrous body. Leaves and branches stuck out through cheeks and nasal passages. Flowers blossomed from open mouths and empty eye sockets. Thick brambles and thorny stalks wound around faces and heads like barbed wire. Head after head, all along the long line of rosebushes. Dozens of them. Some so old, in the ground for so long, they were barely skeletons, mostly old moss and twigs. Fragile. Barely able even to break the surface of the soil.

And then I saw them. Fresh as daisies. Still the color of human flesh, if a slightly greener hue of it. The hick from the country bar. The cowboy. The fat dirtbag who'd felt up Maggie on the dance floor. There he was, a pink rose blooming from his forehead. His eyes were yellowed over, sores accosting his already ugly maw.

And the girl from the Pizza shop. Becca. Her eyebrows were replaced with thorns, her eyes replaced with sharp sticks jutting at odd angles.

They'd come here, hadn't they? After Maggie had kissed them.

"Someone's hungry," Maggie had said in the hick bar as the big ugly redneck walked zombie-like out the door, leaving his friends behind.

Some vague part of my brain thought about the type of scents that certain carnivorous plants used to lure their pray into their traps. Maggie. Her kiss was some kind of lure. Bait to draw people to the farm. They'd driven all the way out here, and for what? For Luke to plant them like flowers?

My mind reeled at the thought of a thing so absurd. I shook free of Luke's grasp and turned to Maggie, my eyes pleading for the horrors in front of us to make sense. "W-what... what is this?"

Her arms were wrapped around herself. Her

shoulders slumped over. She seemed small. Meek. Finally she met my gaze. "You were different, Brian. You aren't like them."

I thought of the look of astonishment on her face after I'd kissed her in the pizza joint. I hadn't turned into a zombie. Didn't drive myself out to my death. But how?

"I'm immune," I said, searching her eyes for our connection, for that thing beyond reason that had drawn me all the way to her. Not her scent. Not a zombie trance. Just *Her.*

"I don't know how. I don't know why you're able to resist it. You gave me one perfect night. One night to feel like a real girl."

She remembered. She would save me now. She would put an end to this madness. I whispered, "Leave with me, Maggie. Leave this all behind."

She wiped her tears away. Her face became cold and uncaring once again. "You should never have come here."

With that, she stepped forward and kicked me into my grave.

The plant people, moaning and crying out in pain, pushed the fresh soil on top of me. Rose petals and cold dirt fell on my face as I screamed.

"It belongs in the garden," Luke said, picking up the shovel he'd stabbed into the dirt. He threw more soil onto my face.

"It belongs in the garden," the plant people echoed back. *"It belongs in the garden. It belongs in the garden."*

"MAGGIE!" I screamed, spitting dirt, trying to scramble to my feet. My throat tore from the intensity of my shouting. Finally I found my footing, sloughed off the dirt and petals piling on top of me. I grabbed the edges of the grave and thrust myself toward her. "MAGGIE, PLEASE!"

How could she do this? I knew STILL that she felt

for me what I felt for her. She STILL loved me, I felt it in my bones. And yet, here I lay, scrambling inside my grave. Fighting for every inch of my life. Fighting to keep her talking to me, even for one last second.

Luke continued to pile dirt on top of me. The plant people surged forward, grabbing hold of my body, dragging me into the garden.

"If you feel nothing when they're gone," she said without emotion, her eyes blank and glazed, "their sacrifice was meaningless."

With that, she pushed me down into the dirt.

As my head sunk beneath the fresh earth, I locked eyes with my love one last time.

She broke her gaze and turned away.

"Just die, Brian."

CHAPTER 12
REVELATION

And so I did die in that bed of roses. The human part of me, anyway. The man part. Brian Sully, cult filmmaker. Famous in the right circles, disgraced pervert in the wrong ones. Dead.

But another part of me, the part that Maggie couldn't explain, the part that was immune to her siren-like scent. Her poison. Whatever it was that lured people to the farm, to their deaths in the rose garden. That part wouldn't die. That part lived.

As the plant people pulled me deeper into the dirt, as the rose petals choked the last vestiges of breath from my lungs, their roots climbed through the soil all around me, wrapping up my arms and legs, twisting around my throat, holding me in place while they buried me alive.

Maggie's blank face, her uncaring eyes, were still imprinted in my mind, trapping me down there in the dark depths of the rose garden with nothing but that awful image to hold onto.

Time passed. How much time?

Pain. Agony shot through my limbs as the root system burrowed into my flesh. Wiry vines pumped white-hot fluid through my veins while other tubers and proboscis sucked my blood and liquid essentials through gouged holes in my face, brain and belly, feeding the root system, providing the garden with sustenance.

"Someone got hungry."

My life was replaced with her life. With Mother.

But unlike the other plant-people, the zombie-things living in the garden—robbed of themselves, robbed of their essence, their personalities, their very being—my consciousness did not abate. No, I did not become a slave like the others, existing only to feed the host. To feed the garden.

That intangible thing inside me that had blocked Maggie's mind-killing scent. That barrier allowed my mind to remain free. It kept my brain somehow alive. It kept me sane.

It allowed me to *see*.

Mother was not from this world. She had drifted for aeons in the dead vacuum of space. Drifting amongst the stars. Nestled deep in a rocky asteroid, safe from decay. Dormant. Dreaming. After countless rotations around our solar system, the asteroid was finally caught in the Earth's gravitational pull, slowly spinning through a degrading orbit until it became an enormous fireball crashing down through our atmosphere in a glorious purple and green explosion that annihilated anything within a ten-mile radius of the blast zone.

It took decades for anything to grow near the crater. But Mother was nothing if not patient. Once the plant and animal life returned, Mother drank from it, assimilated it into her DNA structure. She became what she fed on. Never too greedy. For her kind to survive, she had to be careful not to scare away prey, nor attract predators that would root her up and consume her.

Hundreds of years in the dark earth.

Thousands.

Tens of thousands.

And then man appeared.

They settled the land over which she slept. First with primitive animal skin huts, later with cabins made from the trees. And she fed. Each victim giving up its thoughts. She learned language. Culture.

That's when she sprouted her first drone.

Under the rose garden I seethed and thrashed. My flesh hardened. Bark-like. The last of my blood was sucked from my body, replaced with Mother's milk. The human body was fragile, weak, too quickly depleted of its vital nutrients. Mother needed sustenance like any other organism. By preserving the bodies, keeping them in that zombie-like state under the soil, she was able to feed off of each body for decades or longer, if she was patient enough.

The root system pumping me with her life-essence ran the length and breadth of the entire farm. I could see through the eyes of the goats. Hear the cars passing on the road past the trees. My mind was one with Mother. Her senses. Her feelings. Her memories.

And I wanted more.

I watched through time, through thousands of long-dead eyes as Mother grew drones, perfectly human in every detail. Every detail she needed to lure people back to her. To feed—on their minds as much as their bodies. The more her drones could convincingly interact with the surrounding culture, the more people on which she could feed.

I saw the times Mother had gotten greedy. Fed too much from too small a population. Drones slayed. Her surface blooms and vines destroyed. But she was clever, Mother. She would always find a way to survive, to burrow deeper. To sleep until the time was right. Then she would infect a new host to carry her away somewhere new.

I saw this very farm being built by zombified carpenters. A score of them, plucked from communities far away and spread apart so as not to attract suspicion. Lured by a cute drone with black hair, cropped bangs and big tits named Shaina.

I saw them encasing Mother's delicate petals inside the walls, building the structure around her, encasing her leaves and shoots between brick and drywall, her main arterial stem traversing the fireplace.

When they were finished, I saw them all walk together, single-file, to the rose garden. Saw them dig their own graves, then climb inside. Those men were still down here in the dirt today, rotten, mostly decomposed, mostly useless. Mother has been here, disguised as this farm, for more than a hundred years. She's learned to be patient. To be careful.

I shifted in my grave. I lurched upward, trying to break free from the roots, but they were too strong. I was too weak. They wrapped around me. Through me. Dug tunnels through my muscles. Attached to my bones. The roots are me. I am them.

How long had I been in the ground? Hours? Weeks? Months?

I kept sifting through Mother's memories. Looking for *her*. For my Maggie.

I found Luke.

I saw cars pull down the gravel drive. Saw their occupants fling open doors and shamble to the rose garden. I saw Luke waiting for them with fresh graves. Graves just like mine.

I saw him drive their cars away. Saw him remove all of the evidence that they were ever here. I saw a cop on the porch with a big cowboy hat and shiny belt buckle— Sheriff Ryan Smith. Luke met him at the door. Luke was much smaller than he is now. He had human hands. He didn't talk like a child.

Neighbors reported seeing people drive out to the property. Never saw anyone leave. Could the Sheriff look around? See the farm for himself?

Sure he could. Luke showed him the pigs. Showed him the chickens.

Showed him the rose garden.

Sheriff Smith's grave is to my right. The neighbors' graves are to my left.

Then I saw her.

The moon was high when her pod pushed its way up through the earth behind the house. Luke was there. He helped to carefully break open the pod shell with his human hands, gentle and small. Pale liquid spurted as a translucent sac, spider-webbed with purple veins, oozed out from between the thick green shoots.

Luke pulled the membrane away, taking care not to damage the precious center. Inside, there was a child. Bright green. Slits for eyes, nose and mouth. Barely formed fingers and toes sprouted from its tiny limbs. Luke picked up the child and carried it to the rose garden.

The plant-heads pushed up out of the earth, greeting the new drone with reverence. Luke placed the baby on the ground. Its tiny fingers grew into vines, each finding a plant-head in which to burrow into.

The plant-heads shriveled as the baby sucked the essence from them. Eyes sunk back into skulls and lower mandibles fell away as the heads disintegrated and turned to mush.

The baby grew.

Her hard green body softened. Pink spots appeared, then bloomed, until her entire outer shell became flesh. She grew long. She stood on sure legs. Her beautiful face formed. Her breasts heaved. Her hair turned as red as the rose petals at her feet.

My Maggie was born.

It wasn't that memory that gave me the strength to grab hold of the roots and pull. To dig my feet in and push with every ounce of strength my mutated body possessed. It wasn't that memory of my lover that shot me up through the rich earth, that propelled me out of my grave when no man or woman before me had ever been able to resist the roots of the rose garden.

It wasn't seeing Maggie, my love, that gave me the courage and the will to break my bondage. No, there was something else in those memories. Between the lines. Something inside Mother that she did not want me to see. Something she feared. And now I possessed it.

The knowledge that neither Luke nor Maggie—nor any drone before them—knew.

But me, I was different. I was something in between human and drone, kept alive by the only thing a drone and a human had never shared in all the thousands of years Mother had been on Earth:

True Love. A mingling of drone lure-poison and human will that mutated me and created an entirely new species.

A hybrid. And thus I had conscious access to Mother's hive-mind that they did not. I pulled myself up out of the grasps of all of those plant zombies and broke the wet surface of the garden, because I now knew one thing no one else on this planet had ever known.

I knew how to kill Mother.

NOW

CHAPTER 13
THE HOUSE

The rain crashes down all around me. Lightning and thunder flash and boom, lighting up the sky every other second. I stand naked. Born again in *Her* image. In front of the house. In front of Mother.

My hair writhes, no longer inert at the root. No longer hair at all, but shoot and vine. I feel each individual strand as I would my fingers or my toes. My skin has gone dark—not like the zombies in the soil; dark like bark. Hardening, cracked open in hundreds of places where fresh sprouts, flowers and leaves bloom as my body soaks and absorbs the water droplets crashing all around me.

I am a living rainforest.

I hear the rain smacking against the broken bodies of Luke and Maggie behind me. I know they won't stay down for long. I hear them beginning to stir, beginning to regenerate. I have to work quickly.

I have to kill Mother.

I take a step forward and find that my leg will not move. The roots and vines peppered across my body wriggle and bleed of their own accord. Even detached directly from Mother's body, they are under her control. Everything on this farm is under her control. *Mother is the farm.* The roots in my feet dig into the earth, trapping me in place.

Mother is scared. I smell her fear.

The mangled truck is to my left. I reach out and grab the back gate, wrenching my feet free from the ground. I climb into the truck. Sitting, I rip long strips from the blue tarp covering the front portion of the truck bed. I wrap them around my bare feet, even as the roots shift and squirm. I secure the makeshift shoes in place with cord I find amongst the trash in the back of the truck.

I also find an old rusted ax. And a gas can.

Before I can grab them, I'm flung out of the truck bed, high into the air. I crash down on my face and neck. If I was still a man, the fall would have severed my spine and left me paralyzed, if not dead. But I'm no longer a man, and I no longer have a spine. I have shoots and stems and sticks for bones.

I sit up. Luke's awake.

His human face is gone; I took care of that. He stands over me, some ten feet tall now, his face a mess of split bark, bloody moss and two fierce, yellow glowing eyes.

"Let me guess. You want me back in the garden?" I say, climbing to my feet before the roots in my back and arms can find purchase in the dirt.

Luke lunges, both his gigantic arms longer now than he is tall, his hands the size of barrels, the barbs on the ends of his fingers like kitchen knives.

I duck under his massive swing and hop back up into the truck bed. I grab what I need.

Luke spins around, roaring like a freight train, his mouth growing impossibly large.

"Catch!" I yell, throwing the gas can inside of it.

He rushes forward again, arms back and ready to strike, gas can stuck in his mouth.

I throw the ax as hard as I can, splitting the can down the middle, causing its contents to gush out all over Luke's monstrous face and chest.

That doesn't slow him down a bit. He scales the truck as I leap over the cab, onto the mangled hood. I check back to make sure Luke is giving chase.

He is.

I scramble off the hood and rush for the porch.

He's trailing gasoline as he finally reaches up and yanks the can and ax from his mouth, tossing it behind him.

I chance casting a glance in the direction I had left Maggie. She's gone. I look back at Luke. Too late.

He claws across my chest, knocking me onto the steps. I look down to see pale greenish fluid shooting out of me in great spurts all across the four slash marks I'd received for my trouble. Before he can attack again, I scramble up the steps. "Follow me, fucker!" I yell, kicking the door open, running into the house.

He does.

My wounds are already sealing themselves shut when Luke comes through the doorway.

Slowly, cautiously, I step backward into the living room.

Luke wipes gasoline out of his big glowing eyes. He has to duck to clear the archway. He's getting bigger the angrier he gets.

Good. I need him big.

Gasoline fumes hang heavy in the air as he picks up the wooden rocking chair from the corner.

"Hit me, you big motherfucker! Hit me as hard as you can!"

He obliges. I take the chair full-force in the face. I fly backward, slamming into the wall. If I still breathed air like normal people, it would have been knocked out of me, with a few fractured ribs for good measure. I land in a crumpled heap behind the couch while the chair splinters to pieces.

Luke stalks forward, picking up the couch I'm lying behind. He holds it over his head, ready to smash down and turn me into a green smear on the hardwood floor.

That's when I do it.

I have matches in my hand. A big box of wooden matches. I'd snatched them from the fireplace when I ran through the door. I strike one, drop it in the box, causing the others to ignite. I throw it at Luke's chest.

Then I run.

He goes up fast. He's old. That crumbling bark-like skin. All that dry moss, sticks and twigs. It burns big.

He drops the couch, but it's too late. It's already caught fire as well. He drops it right onto the splintered chair. Perfect kindling. In moments, the entire living room is engulfed, the huge flames licking the tall ceiling.

I dash into the kitchen. I throw down the hutch in the doorway before the flaming monster can give chase. Dishes smash against the floor. I flip the heavy wooden table onto it, creating a barrier while I finish what I need to do.

It only lasts a second. Flaming wood explodes around me as I get to the stove. I duck down, only taking a few big pieces to the back while I yank the knobs on the front, turning the gas on high. I raise up and flip the oven to broil, when Luke grabs me.

He's so fucking hot I have to shield my face from his flames as he picks me up. He screams in my face, but his mouth can no longer form words. His tongue is just roaring flames, his throat white-hot embers.

His hands and arms fall apart, sending me crashing to the floor before I, too, catch fire. If it wasn't for my body being soaked in all of the wet rain and pulpy tree-sap blood having just shot out of me when Luke slashed my chest open, I might have been just as crispy as him.

Instead I escape barely singed. I scurry through the flaming rubble, past the front door and down the porch steps.

Just as I clear the final step, the house explodes.

The blast sends me clear across the yard. I land in a heap, my body blackened. Thick gray smoke rolls off me for a moment before I begin to regenerate.

The root tendrils across my body no longer work against me. Mother is too preoccupied with burning alive to worry about controlling me any longer.

I sit in the grass with a grin on my face as the farmhouse smolders.

Pieces of roof collapse onto the second floor. Support beams melt under the intense heat. I start to see Mother's true form as the flaming house falls away. It starts with a shudder, then she shakes violently back and forth, trying to rid herself of the pain searing her flesh. The brick walls on the east side crumble, revealing a pair of beautiful red petals. The front of the house falls away, allowing her huge leaves to unfurl. They're scorched and blackened. Smoke blooms into the night sky as the rain continues to fall, helping to ease Mother's burns, but not strong enough to squelch the inferno blazing below.

That's when I hear her scream.

Maggie.

"No!" I leap to my feet. I run forward as fast as I can.

Maggie's in the house.

CHAPTER 14
MAGGIE'S A MONSTER

I slide to a halt when I see her standing in what's left of the archway of the front door. The inferno screams behind her. She's standing in the middle of the fire, but it does not consume her.

She steps out of the house. She's still young, her insides still dense, thick, green. She doesn't burn like her brother. She bleeds, thick and green. Blood sizzles out of her arms and chest. Thick smoke escapes her nose and mouth. But she does not burn.

"She liked you, Brian." Maggie's hair fans out in waves, thick tendrils swaying this way and that. Like cobras ready to strike. Her yellow eyes are bright. "She liked the way you tasted when she ate your cum. She told me it was sweet."

The moss-woman from my dream. No dream at all, it turns out. "I fucked your mother. How awkward."

Ignoring my quip, Maggie descends the front steps. Her blood no longer boils. Her body no longer smokes. She heals fast. "She would have let you walk off this farm. The only human to ever survive a night here. Do you know how special that is? How special you are?"

"You still kicked me in the dirt. Buried me alive," I say, walking toward her. I ball my fists and flex the roots jutting from my flesh. I feel myself gaining full control over my new body.

We meet face to face in the middle of the yard. She's taller than me now. Her human flesh is all gone.

"You're still beautiful, ya know? Even green and... kinda pointy."

Razor sharp thorns crisscross her tits. Her flat nose is nothing more than a pair of slits. Her lips are still full, still red as the devil's cock. "Your hair... Well, your hair is kind of freaking me out. Got that Medusa thing going on."

She smirks. "You don't look bad yourself, Brian Sully. Plant monster looks good on you."

I laugh. "We've still got it, don't we?"

"How did you do it? How are you still alive?"

"Because I love you."

Maggie laughs. Her voice is much deeper. "Do you even know why I didn't fuck you that night in the hotel room? Look at me. Do you think I get a period?" She taps her crotch with her finger. "I don't even have a fucking vagina, Brian. I'm a drone. I serve one purpose. You can't love me any more than you can love a honey bee. I do a job. I attract food for Mother. And when I can't produce anymore pheromones, I die. Then another drone replaces me. That's how this works." She hesitates, unsure of her words. She repeats them. "You can't love me."

"You love me, too."

She's silent, her expression blank. She doesn't deny it. "Do you know what happens to us? To Mother's drones after a few seasons? Luke didn't start off dumb. He was just like me only five or six summers ago. We aren't meant to last, Brian. I'm going to grow like he did. I'm going to act and sound like he did. Another young, sexy drone full of venom will take my place and I'll bury the bodies and hide the cars, rambling like a retard as my brain slowly turns to mulch until it's time to return to Mother forever. Could you love that?"

I don't answer.

Behind her, the last of the burning house falls away. Mother's petals unfurl, letting the beating rain put out the last of the flames surrounding her. Inside the gargantuan flower, thousands of eyeballs turn their attention on me. Below them, row after row of pointed brambles and thorns line the interior of her form like a barbed throat. She screams loud enough to shake the ground.

"Mom says hi."

"I don't think she likes me anymore."

Maggie's expression changes. She bares her sharp teeth, sets her fingers into claws. "This is my home, Brian. She's my mother. I can't let you take her from me. And I can't let you leave here to tell the world about us. You have to die."

Before I can respond, she dives forward, pumping her arms back and forth, darting her claws into my chest, causing me to stagger backward. I grunt, taking each shot with full power. Fluid leaks from dozens of holes.

"I won't fight you, Maggie."

"Good. You'll die quicker," she says, standing her ground.

All around us, the farm animals have gathered. The goats and pigs, the chickens. Each a comically mutated version of what I'd seen upon my arrival. The goats stand as tall as horses, the pigs as wide as cars, all of them shot through with vegetation. Not real mammals—plants made to look like real farm stock. Just more façade. More camouflage to hide Mother from the normal world.

Even the Venus flytraps and pitcher plants, now grown to enormous size, have crawled out of the greenhouse to join the cavalcade of horrors.

The new wounds on my chest seal up. "You're gonna have to do better than–"

They explode outward again as tiny barbs Maggie's

talons had left in my chest expand, blowing my chest cavity open, sending both my arms flying into the yard.

The animal monsters cackle and howl as my body parts squirm on the ground, unable to regenerate without close proximity to the host body.

I drop to my knees, eyes wide. Shocked.

Maggie approaches and raises one arm into the air. The nails grow to four times their length, becoming small swords on her hand. "You're right. I do still love you. If things were different—if I wasn't a monster—we could have been great together. Had a life. A family."

"I fucking hate kids," I say, waiting for the killing blow. "But for you? Hey, anything's possible."

With that, she brings her arm down, slashing horizontally across what remains of my chest, cleaving my torso from my lower half.

I slide forward into the grass.

She turns, fingers shrinking back to normal size, and walks back toward the giant rose with eyes and mouths that was once a house. She walks back toward Mother, leaving me for dead. "I'm so sorry for all of this. I wish... I wish I would have never met you."

"Yes," I sputter, pale fluid leaving from my mouth, gushing from every other part of me.

She pauses. "What?"

"Yes," I manage. Finally answering her question. "...I can love you."

Maggie starts to cry.

Behind her, Mother roars, swaying back and forth. *Finish it.* She's saying. *Kill him now.*

Maggie turns to face the enormous creature before her. "I can't, Mother! I love him! I really do! I won't!"

The huge flower bends at its stem, swooping down until it hangs over Maggie, all thousands of those eyes trained on her.

"He's mine, Mother. I want to be with him. I want to leave here. I want a life with–"

A dozen tongue-like vines dart out and wind around Maggie's head, arms and chest. They yank back, pulling her into Mother's razor-lined gullet.

Maggie screams as Mother constricts her petals, ripping her to pieces, swallowing her down. Eating my Maggie.

It's then, in that horrible moment, that blackness overtakes me. I'm bleeding out. There is not enough fluid left inside me to keep me awake. The last thing I hear is the horrible crunch of Maggie's flesh as Mother consumes her.

After that, Darkness takes hold.

CHAPTER 15
A MAGGIE LIFE

My mind returns to that night when Luke helped little Maggie break open the pod. I saw again as her small green form became pink and, in the span of hours, she grew into the shape of a grown woman. She looked nothing like Maggie yet—she didn't look like anyone. Her features were vague, her breasts lacked nipples, her fingers lacked nails. But, while her body was grown, her mind was not.

At first, she couldn't walk. She scuttled around on all fours, not straying far from the garden. She sucked the life out of many plant-heads in her first weeks. Not because her body needed the sustenance—she was already strong and thick, her sinews and shoots able to withstand the worst this world had to offer (drones were nearly impossible to kill when they were first born).

No, it was her brain that needed to eat.

Drones' minds are empty when they're born. They are nothing more than an ambulatory representation of Mother's will, no more capable of mimicking the language and mannerisms of humans than the fake pigs or chickens on the fake farm.

I know this because Mother knows this. And I know everything Mother knows.

I watch as Luke brings a steady stream of poisoned humans onto the farm for Maggie to feed on.

Luke has already lost his drone companion, a blonde woman Mother named Theresa. She'd grown huge and dumb, unable to drive the cars off of the property any longer. Luke had chopped her up and returned her to Mother only a week prior to Maggie's birth.

As of now, he's pulling double duty as both the lure and the planter. But he's already growing. Already getting darker and harder.

Maggie waits by the garden, still naked, still hardly walking on two legs. The poisoned people march right up to her and my love takes them in her arms, gently caressing their bodies as her hair-tendrils—still lacking their red pigmentation—suck out their eyes and their brains, dropping their husks into the garden.

Each time she feeds, she learns more about our world, about our language and customs, as she absorbs the memories of everyone she eats.

That's when Luke walks the woman into the garden.

I feel a jolt as I recognize the woman I love, only she's glassy-eyed and slack-jawed. She walks up to Maggie and smiles, like all of the poisoned people before her. Like every person a Mother-drone has ever kissed—except for me.

When Maggie leans forward and takes the red-haired woman into her arms, snakes her tendrils out and consumes the woman's essence, something changes.

The tendrils take on the size, shape and color of the woman's hair. They become voluminous curls, stark red against Maggie's pale skin. Her face steals the woman's features, leaving the once-beautiful person a shallow-cheeked husk.

Maggie's breasts grow large and her pink nipples sprout. Her ass forms, her waist narrows. Even the tattoos on the woman's arms appear on Maggie's flesh.

Your tattoos. They look like Deep Ones. The shit from my movies.

I don't know what you're talking about. I drew these.

Maggie tosses the woman into the garden. Her used-up form sinks into the soil as Maggie picks her clothes up off the ground. She slides into them effortlessly, her body now an exact replica of her latest victim.

Her body and her mind are complete. My Maggie, my life, is truly born.

I keep watching her. I see her first victims as a lure. I let the memories from Mother's mind play out, taking in as many scenes of Maggie's life as possible. I watch all of it the way Mother watched all of mine while I was in the garden. I will the memories to be slow. I never want them to end.

And then I see them.

The pervert from the bar.

Becca from the pizza shop.

I see the night I met Maggie.

Luke's lumbering, gloved form guides them to the garden where they dutifully bury themselves with no protest. I watch Luke drive their cars away, disposing of all evidence of their arrival. The night wears on and morning shows its face.

I watch with patience, knowing what will happen next.

Then she appears. Maggie. Returned home. I was probably still asleep in the hotel room when she made her way back to Mother. A job well done.

But Maggie does not look pleased with her work. She does not look happy at all. She marches up to the front of the house and sits down in the grass.

My Maggie begins to cry.

"Something happened, Mother. Something bad."

Mother searches her memories, plays back our meeting. Our impossible kiss. Our love-making in the hotel.

Mother grows anxious. She grows furious with Maggie for not killing me. For leaving me with her poison mingling inside of me, starting the process of mutation that would eventually see me rise up from the rose garden.

"I couldn't, Mother. I just couldn't. Not him. He's... different from the others. I think... I think I love him."

My heart aches as I hear her words. I was probably frantically searching the hotel for her at that moment, playing our whole night back to figure out what I'd done wrong to make her leave me. Now I know—she had no choice.

"I'm lonely here, Mother. Luke's time is almost up. He can't even talk right anymore. It's just... I want... I want to be with Brian. I want to leave the farm."

Mother's anger turns white-hot. Maggie cries out as Mother's mental pain surges through her.

"You foolish child! How will you find him now? He could be anywhere! He's got my essence running through his veins! What if it changes him? What if the humans learn of our existence because of him? You've put our life in jeopardy! You've made me vulnerable! I should absorb you right now and start over with a brand new drone!"

As Maggie sobs, I yearn to hold her in my hands. She's close, and yet I cannot comfort her. She seems so alive. So real.

And then I feel it.

Or rather, I feel it wink away. Maggie's essence. Back in the real world. In the present time. Only now do I realize I've felt Maggie's life force this whole time. Ever since the night we kissed and made love.

Its absence is like a vacuum. A void.

My Maggie is gone.

She's dead.

CHAPTER 16
THE HORDE

As consciousness floods my mind, bringing me back to reality, I roar. I don't bother forming words—words are too good for Mother. For this beast, this stealer of my love. Anger and madness tear through me as my eyes burn yellow.

Mother's animals form a line of defense between her and me.

"Do you think you can stop me?!" I scream, writhing on the ground, limbless, still gushing the thin, pale liquid that now passes for my blood.

I will drag myself into that giant flower by my teeth if I have to. Maggie will be mine.

A goat-thing runs forward, rears up and drops its barb-ringed hooves down on top of my prone, limbless form.

I let the beast sink its legs right through what's left of my torso, absorbing the pain, letting it fuel my hatred for the goat-thing's master. It bleats and flails, but it's caught fast; my wounds seal up around its legs, trapping it in place.

Then it's my turn.

The hanging bits of my green flesh turn into tendrils. They wind their way up the goat-thing's legs, its chest. They strangle it, dragging it down to the grass with me. Its yellow eyes are wild as it cries and struggles, thrashing its head back and forth.

I pull my torso on top of it and twist around, using my shattered and splintered rib cage as a grinder, pulverizing its face, assimilating it into my own flesh. Beside me, on the ground, my left arm lays mostly intact. My right is useless, in too many pieces to reconstruct. Vines from my shoulder snake out, grab hold of my good arm and pull it back to my body.

I rise up on four legs. On goat legs.

Mother bellows again, commanding her horde to attack. One of the car-sized pigs breaks forward into a full run, coming at me with the speed of a runaway train.

I raise up onto my haunches. My underside becomes a dense forest of spines. As the hog crashes into me, I slam down on it, squashing its green flesh in an instant. It lays twitching under me, and just as Maggie had absorbed the woman she would become, I make the hog's flesh my own, growing my size.

Behind me, I hear moaning.

The plant-heads have risen from the grave. They shamble out from behind the greenhouse. Mother is attacking with everything she's got. But she's weak, burned, damaged. I'm strong, and growing stronger by the second.

In front of me, a giant flytrap with jaws the size of trashcan lids slithers forward, using its roots for locomotion. It stands as tall as me.

As it strikes, I grab it around the stem and yank it off the ground. Spinning it around, I jam its roots into my exploded right shoulder, fashioning myself another arm.

I turn to face the plant-heads. Sheriff Smith and the dirtbag cowboy lead the stumbling zombies. Becca the pizza girl is right behind them.

"Stop!" I command, reaching out to them with my mind, not yet sure if I'm strong enough to telepathically control the farm the way Mother does.

To my surprise, the plant-heads do as I say. My human DNA seems to be in tune with theirs. I grin and turn back, facing the farm animals blocking my path to Mother and the giant plants continuously flooding from the greenhouse.

I try the same mental trick with the plant army. No good. Mother's creations are firmly under her control.

A pair of pitcher plants lunge forward, and a dozen dog-sized green chickens cluck their way toward me. I ride by, grabbing up one of the pitcher plants—a thick, tree of a thing that was even taller than me—as I do so.

I will my plant-head forces to advance as I rip the writhing stem from the huge pitcher plant, leaving only its cup full of liquid intact.

When the chicken-things get near, I fling the contents of the pitcher on them, its acidic compounds dissolving them instantly.

The rest of the animal-things charge forward, meeting my plant-head brigade head on, the two weird armies smashing, slashing, biting, chomping and splashing either other to a slimy pulp.

Sheriff Smith (what's left of him after so much time in the garden, anyway) climbs onto the back of a truck-sized hog. Three other plant-heads follow suit. Using his stripped-to-the-bone fingers, the Sheriff digs deep gouges into the hog's green skin, causing an eruption of pale fluid. The other plant-heads swarm the wound, ripping it open, feasting on the flesh of the huge beast as it tries in vain to shake them free.

As it falls dead, Sheriff Smith and his plant-heads move on to the next mutated farm animal, then the next, felling most of the monsters creating the barrier between myself and Mother.

Elsewhere, Becca the pizza girl is being eaten by a

giant flytrap. Her legs kick uselessly as the hippo-sized monstrosity sits patiently, content to let the plant-head zombie girl dissolve inside its maw while the rest of the chaotic battle rages around it.

Suddenly, Becca's arms smash through the top of the giant plant's upper trap hinge. Flailing and scratching, she tears herself free, standing triumphant with fists full of flytrap gore as the huge thing falls over dead.

The plant-heads are winning, but more and more writhing, pulpy things sprout from the ground all around the burned-out husk of the house, wrapping themselves around the decaying zombies, dragging them to the ground.

I lose my patience. I have to get to Maggie.

I turn to the hulking alien plant in front of me. "Give her to me!" I scream. "Let us go and you can live! We'll leave you in peace!"

As a response, Mother folds her petals up tight, closing herself off to me.

Screaming in frustration, I race through the pack of plant-zombies and vegetable creatures, shredding them all violently as I pass, until I get to the truck. Grabbing it with my flytrap arm, I heave it into the air and fling it at the giant flower.

I don't wait for it to hit before I dig my hooves into the earth and charge toward the alien monster.

The truck smashes into Mother's petals, tearing a hole near her stem, causing her to scream out in pain. Before she can regenerate, before she can close the hole, I dive through, my body torn to shreds as I pass by the barbed teeth.

As I descend into the belly of Mother.

As I race to find my Maggie.

CHAPTER 17
INSIDE

My bleeding body lands in the dark. Down here—inside Mother's belly—is a vast network of tunnels. She is cyclopean in size—the flower that blooms above the earth is a mere fraction of her total mass.

"Maggie!" I yell out, trying to find my lost love.

I hear my voice echo through chamber after chamber. Mother has grown in this spot for hundreds of years—plenty of time to lay long, labyrinthine root systems. A lesser man would be lost down here in the dark forever.

My eyes blaze yellow, lighting my way.

Tall columns of purple and pink sinew hold up the interior of the dark red roots. Sinister shadows play across the circular tubes as I wander from one tunnel to the next. A normal human would go mad walking through the spiraling shapes and endless corridors.

But I have something other men do not.

I have Maggie. I have love.

But is she still alive? Am I too late?

And then, impossibly, as I round a tall bend in the endless cavern, I come upon her.

Maggie.

Whole. Alive. Waiting for me.

"I wasn't sure you'd make it," she says, embracing me.

"Oh, Maggie," I whisper into her hair, wrapping my arms around her. "How did you survive? I was sure you were lost to me forever."

"It doesn't matter," she says softly. "We can leave."

"What?" I say, astonished.

"Mother says I can go. Just take me. Take me out of here, and we can be together just like you wanted."

Just like you wanted.

I pull back, staring deeply into Maggie's eyes. They're perfect. Just like I remember them. Her hair, her smell, her lips. They all belong to my beautiful Maggie.

I reach out and caress her face. Then I smash it to pieces.

Maggie shatters like glass. Hollow. A copy. An illusion.

I drop my haunches, the fingers of my humanoid hand turning to vines as I dig them into the soft skin that makes up the chamber before me. Closing my eyes, I invade Mother's mind.

She appears before me in the dark. The same beautiful moss-faced visage that made love to me on my first night on the farm.

I admire your tenacity, Brian Sully. You're a hard man to kill. But you are just a man.

"I'm going to kill you. Give Maggie to me. Then you die."

Mother laughs high and shrill, the sound of it echoing through the chamber.

I do not die. I am forever.

I search her mind while she talks, racing through the labyrinth as fast as my mind can travel, through every dark twist and pitch black curve.

"We'll see about that."

I know what you are doing. You won't find her. You'll never find her. She is my drone. My seed. Mine to keep, and mine to kill. You have no rights to my kind. We are star children. You are just an abhorrent freak of nature. An abomination soon snuffed out. A mistake never to be made again.

I know she won't let me see Maggie in her mind. I'm not looking for Maggie.

I stall, talking to her to keep her busy. "Maggie told me you were going to let me leave. Why? I was infected with your poison. You said it would change me. Why would you ever let me go once you had me here?"

I lied. She loved you. I could not let her know that you were doomed the moment she kissed you in that pizza parlor.

There. I see it, finally.

I retract my fingers and charge ahead into the tunnel directly before me.

In that instant, Mother realizes what I've found.

NO! she screams. Her face vanishes. She's going to try to beat me to it.

The root system collapses ahead.

I smash through the wall to my left, punching through the solid earth with my trap hand, slashing my way into the next root with the clawed fingers of my humanoid hand.

I storm through the barriers as fast as she can form them, ever deeper, down into the innermost depths of her monolithic form. And then I arrive.

Her heart chamber.

It hangs there, beating. Brilliant purple. The essence of life radiating from its center, lighting up the whole room in glorious violet hues. It's no larger than a human heart, yet somehow beats strong enough to shake the entire room, strung up with thousands of fibers and filaments running in every direction, sending vital fluids all through Mother's entire titanic body.

She's dead.

Mother walks into the heart chamber behind me, carrying a lifeless form.

I turn to face her.

Maggie dangles from Mother's mossy arms—what's left of her, anyway. Her lower half and right arm are gone, ripped apart in Mother's mouth when she swallowed my love. Maggie's tendril hair hangs limp. Her yellow eyes are dim. She's gone. My lover is gone.

Mother drops her to the floor. She's shaking. She puts her long, slender arms out in front of her. *Take her. Take her and go. She's yours. Bury her. Mourn her. Just leave me be!*

My rage cannot be contained. I bare my teeth. Yellow flames rise up out of my eye sockets. I turn and grab the heart by its life-strings.

Noooooo!!!

I rip the heart from its mooring, causing the entire massive structure to shake. The violet light goes out. The room turns a brackish brown before my eyes. Pale fluid jets from the hanging veins like spoiled milk. The chamber begins to collapse.

Give it back to me! Mother screams, the mossy face of her humanoid avatar already beginning to crumble.

I hold the heart out in my open hand. As Mother lunges toward me, I close my fist around her precious life force and punch a hole through the middle of her face, screaming in anguish.

I drop to my haunches, weeping. I shake the corpse of Mother from my hand. I pull Maggie close to me. Her mouth hangs open. Her eyes rolled up, unfocused.

"Come back to me," I cry, pushing the tendril hair out of her face. "Come back, my love."

I push my vine-like fingers through her skull, into her brain. Searching. Searching for even a tiny spark of life.

I find none.

Finally, with Mother decaying all around me, crumbling, falling in huge chunks, I sling Maggie's body across my back and run.

Up. Up through the maze of bleeding, dying, rotting flesh. Up toward the normal world. A world to which I no longer belong.

A world without Maggie.

CHAPTER 18
FOREVER

When I finally crawl out of Mother's dead husk, dawn has broken. The rain has stopped. Her vegetable creatures lay in pools of pale gunk; her plant-head zombies in crumpled heaps. A fresh dew anoints the grass, and normal Earthly insects cry out—in mourning for my lost love?

I lay Maggie on the ground, still weeping. Small purple flowers bloom from her mangled torso.

"Still trying to live. Even in death."

I pause.

Opening my hand, I find that I still hold Mother's heart. It still glows with life. Quickly, I break open Maggie's chest and lay the heart inside. I hold my breath. I wait.

Nothing happens.

I use my tendril fingertips to dig into the heart, then out the other side. I bury my fingers into Maggie's own heart, acting as a conduit. With the palm of my hand I smash down on Mother's heart, causing it to briefly glow brighter, causing Maggie's one remaining limb to convulse.

Nothing.

I do it again. "Live! Live!"

Nothing.

Sobbing, I retract my fingers.

"I will not live on this Earth without you!"

I climb to my feet. "I will burn myself to cinders! I will join you in oblivion!"

Dragging a smoldering piece of wall from the smoking rubble of the house, I build a pyre. Before long it roars to life.

I return to Maggie. I pick her up into my arms, hugging her tight. I kiss her as deeply, as passionately as the night we met. The night we fell in love. A man and a monster. Earth and stars. My face melts, joins hers. Her body absorbs into mine. Mother's heart beats in my chest. I turn to the pyre. I prepare to leap inside.

You'll burn yourself to cinders and join me in oblivion? A bit melodramatic, don't you think, Brian Sully? What is this, one of your crappy B-movies?

"MAGGIE!" I cry aloud.

In the flesh... Well, in your flesh. Ours, I guess. This might take some getting used to. Do we have to have goat legs?

I drop again to my haunches, screaming in joy. "I thought I'd lost you. I thought you were gone forever!"

And let you throw yourself into a fire for me? Never.

I laugh and laugh as the sound of distant sirens fills the air.

We should probably leave, unless you want to explain to the police why you killed my mother and burned down her house... And why we're an otherworldly plant-monster.

"How are we getting out of here? We could have left hours ago if you hadn't have ripped the steering wheel off the truck like some kind of she-hulk."

At least I didn't run it out of gas.

We walk toward the treeline. "It's a nice morning.

Let's just see where it takes us."

I'm good with that.

Scores of fire trucks and police cars race up the gravel drive as we pass into the trees.

"Hey," the me part of us asks, miles away from Mother's farm, from the nightmare of the night before. "Can we name our first drone Conan?"

We are not naming our first drone Conan!

"Damn."

THAT NIGHT IN THE HOTEL ROOM

"What's your favorite part of the farm? You told me about the animals, the hard work. But out of everything you do there everyday, what's the thing you like the most about it?"

She considered my question for a long while, tracing lines in my belly hair, twirling it up on her fingers, then letting it spring back down into wet curly Q's. "Honestly?" she asked, returning my gaze. "The trees. The trees are my favorite part."

"Trees? Trees are everywhere. What's so special about the trees on your farm?"

"Not just the trees on my farm. All trees. Trees are free."

"How are trees free? They never move."

"The seeds. They blow away. They travel with the winds, get picked up by birds or little animals. They end up far, far away from where they started. Then they put down roots and start anew. They make a home in a faraway land, and the cycle starts all over again."

About The Author

Kevin Strange is a two time nominee of the Wonderland Book Award for excellence in bizarro fiction, and recipient of the 2014 editors choice award in the Lewis and Clark college literary magazine The Peppermint Rooster Review. He is the author of 14 books and the writer/director of 7 films. He loves schlocky B-movies, cult fiction and Iron Maiden records.

"All The Toxic Waste From My Heart"

Since 2012 Kevin Strange has been smashing medulla oblongatas with his unique brand of horror and bizarro fiction. He returns here with a brand new collection of short stories sure to leave readers recreationally deranged or at the very least psychotically inclined. All The Toxic Waste From My Heart features ten brain-bending tales ranging from the whimsical fantasy of a boy who falls in love with a whale fart to an apocalyptic wasteland full of cannibalistic sludge monsters. Fans of Strange know that he only gets better and weirder with time. And ALL THE TOXIC WASTE FROM MY HEART proves to be no different.

"Texas Chainsaw Mantis"

Praying Mantises have evolved into the dominant species on Earth, having wiped out humans years ago after a genetic experiment evolved the species into man-sized, super intelligent insects. But they don't just roam the planet aimlessly. The Mantises have taken over our jobs. Kept the generators running, the oil pumping, and the economy in place. They're people, just like us ...Except that they're cannibalistic, blood thirsty nymphomaniacs who love biting the heads off their partners while they mate. Part Texas Chainsaw Massacre, part Evil Dead, pray this mantis doesn't find you next!

Now Available at KevinTheStrange.com!

"Computerface"

While the Machines ravage humanity in a horrific, prolonged and violent genocide, the survivors of this nightmare apocalyptic world spend their short, miserable lives hiding and running, doing their best to avoid the giant torture robots and man-sized retrieval units. That is, until they find Computerface, a man with an iPad grafted to his face. This bizarre disfigurement confuses the robot retrieval units, giving the human survivors an upper hand against the robots for the first time since their uprising. But will Computerface become the hero this decimated world needs, or will he remain the selfish sociopath he'd been in his former life?

"Murder Stories for your Brain Piece"

A gateway to another dimension buried deep inside a disembodied rectum. Scavengers who achieve immortality by sewing themselves into new bodies. A woman obsessed with having sex with the Loch Ness Monster. These tales, and more, comprise the second collection from Bizarro Fiction workhorse, Kevin Strange. These seven stories follow his acclaimed 2013 collection, The Last Gig on Planet Earth and other Strange Stories, and promise to be more violent, more horrific, and more bizarre than anything he's published yet. Let's get weird, gang. Let's get strange.

Now Available at KevinTheStrange.com!

"Vampire Guts in Nuke Town"

Guts is a bad motherfucker in a bad, bad world. In Nuke Town, Guts wakes up in a strange motel with no memory of how he got there. A brother and sister duo are the only two humans in sight, but are they friend or foe? As the paranoia sets in, and Guts begins to understand the true implications of a nest of sophisticated, mutated vampires, he must use all the cunning and skills that his years in the wasteland have taught him if he hopes to survive the horror that awaits him in … Vampire Guts in Nuke Town!

"Robamapocalypse"

In a dystopian future where Barack Obama is lord and emperor of the only city left on earth after the zombie apocalypse, one young man must fight his way through a tournament pitting zombie against remote controlled zombie if he hopes to stop the evil, half-cyborg dictator from destroying Steel City and the rest of the fabled Obamamerica beyond. Time traveling terrorists, giant robot zombies made of zombies, and Barack Obama like you've never seen him before are but a few of the twists and turns that make Robamapocalypse one of the weirdest, most action packed bizarro stories you'll ever lay your unsuspecting eyeballs on.

This election year, Barack Obama is a giant fucking robot.

Now Available at KevinTheStrange.com!

"Cotton Candy"

Mr. P was just your average, ordinary junior college English professor, that is until his wife unexpectedly dies. Without his moral compass to guide him, Mr. P soon spirals into a pit of despair, indulging in every form of fleshy carnality his 62 year old mind can imagine. After learning of a secret gangbang party from a flyer found at his local porn shop, Mr. P embarks on a bizarre journey involving midgets with huge cocks, female-to-male transgender bangers, and a hostess whose kinks involve more than just dressing up like a giant stuffed animal. Has Mr. P bitten off more than he can chew? Will his perversions prove fatal? Find out in this novella by Hardcore Bizarro virtuoso Kevin Strange.

"The Humans Under the Bed"

500 years after monsters wiped out the human race, a quiet calm has settled over the population of nightmare creatures that go bump in the night. They work their monster jobs, raise their monster families, tend to their monster homes, and generally enjoy the peace and prosperity of life without their sworn enemies, the human scourge, that so blighted the land for so many centuries. Until now....

"The Last Gig on Planet Earth and Other Strange Stories"

Kevin Strange's fiction has been described as bleak, hopeless, bizarre, and always unpredictable. This is Strange at his most nihilistic. The Last Gig on Planet Earth collects seven tales full of suspense, of dread, of that side of human nature that most pretend does not exist. Strange sets his spotlight directly in its gnarled face and demands it reveal its most twisted secrets.

"McHumans"

After Cthulhu awakens and destroys civilization as we know it, humans are used as slaves and food by their new slimy, submerged masters. One such young man, Ricky, works at an undersea fast food joint where he's forced to kill and cook other humans for the Deep Ones to eat. But he has a plan. His restaurant caters to the Big Man himself, and if Ricky's plan works, he could pull off the unthinkable:

He could actually Kill Cthulhu.

Now Available at KevinTheStrange.com!

Made in the USA
Lexington, KY
05 March 2017